Contents

The Porpoise and the Otter

The Porpoise and the Otter

The Literary Friendship of
Max Beerbohm and G.K. Chesterton

William Blissett

Rock's Mills Press
Oakville, Ontario
2022

Published by
Rock's Mills Press
www.rocksmillspress.com

The drawings on the cover are details from pen-and-ink self-caricatures done by Beerbohm and Chesterton in 1909. They were discovered in an autograph album by Anton C. Masin, archivist, who reproduced them in *The Chesterton Review* 5, no. 1 (Fall–Winter 1978–1989) from the original sketches in the University of Notre Dame's Chesterton Collection. The Beerbohm sketch is flipped horizontally for design purposes. We thank the representatives for the Beerbohm and Chesterton literary estates for permission to reproduce the images.

For information about this book, including permissions, trade orders, and bulk orders, please contact the publisher at customer.service@rocksmillspress.com.

Preface

Let me start with the story of my interest and delight in these two figures on the literary scene over many decades. It is a simple fact – neither a boast nor a confession – that in my youth I was a deft performer on examinations. One dodge I hit upon, crass in motive but canny, was to immerse myself in reading some rapid, pointed, stylish treatment of tomorrow's examination field. While yet an undergraduate, the first abettor for "the Victorian age in literature" was G.K. Chesterton. Having picked up his little book for its sober title, I read it at a sitting and went the next day rollicking into the examination room. A few years later, as a graduate student, one of my cherished mentors was Norman Endicott, who "always had a phrase," whether of Sir Thomas Browne, whom he edited, or of Max Beerbohm. How well he would have fitted into that little group of Max's friends who met annually on his birthday and called themselves the Maximilians. The scenes and captions of *Rossetti and his Circle* and others of Max's scenes and captions gave me a fistful of winners to play on the Departmental Examination on the Victorians and early Moderns.

Years pass, the doctorate arrives, and academic appointment. I came to know the artist and poet David Jones and some of his circle. One of his executors, René Hague, with his wife, Joan, a daughter of Eric Gill, belonged to English Catholic culture of the mid-twentieth century; I saw what it was to have Chesterton's books scattered about and to recall his quips and notions and fictions and the serious jollity of his controversies. Another friend must be named – Douglas Cleverdon, with his wife, Nest – "pretty Nest like apple blossom," to appropriate a line from Welsh poetry. Douglas began in the book business, a champion of fine printing and publisher of illustrated books, most notably Jones's celebrated *Ancient Mariner* – in two editions from the same plates, fifty years apart. He moved on to be a producer of "features" for the B.B.C. – Jones's *In Parenthesis*, Dylan Thomas's *Under Milk Wood*, and Max Beerbohm's radio talks, including the most famous two, in 1942, at the nadir of the War, one on "Advertisements" and one on "Music Halls of my Youth," in which the old gentleman sang snatches, including one of his own composition. It was said at the time that the two great masters of radio and builders of morale were Churchill and Max.

My own interest and liking grew, and I found myself writing the piece on "Max Beerbohm the Essayist" for the *Dictionary of Literary Biography* and serving as an advisory editor of *The Chesterton Review*. In 1987, at a conference in Seattle on C.S. Lewis and G.K. Chesterton, I gave a talk on G.K.C. and Max, brightened with illustrative slides. It was published with the other papers in *The Riddle of Joy* (Michael H. Macdonald and Andrew A. Tadie, ed., Grand Rapids, MI.: Eerdmans, 1989). The present study, redrafted six years later, is six times its length.

"Study?" Samuel Johnson observed that a man may turn over half a library to make one book; so it has been here. The centenary first of Max and then of G.K. has come and gone. To enter the world of literary history and of the history of ideas, as both our writers have done, is to be subject to retrieval, citation, annotation, commentary. Max attended Merton College, Oxford, and walked away without taking a degree. G.K.C. entered the Slade School of Fine Art in London and seems to have left no record of any kind. To say with certainty that neither of them ever composed a proper footnote would necessitate my turning again a thousand pages of Max's writing and ten thousand of G.K.C.'s – a game not worth the candle. I promise, instead, to keep my own footnotes down.

It is not easy to settle the arrangement of a book about two apparently disparate writers who knew each other for more than thirty years but met only occasionally, did not exchange letters and were not linked either by close friendship or obsessive rivalry. Fortunately, how they first came to know each other and what each brought to the meeting can be ascertained; and the major role of someone very like Max in Chesterton's first novel, *The Napoleon of Notting Hill*, will demand a close look, and so the first two chapters take their place. In the third we find them doing a highly Victorian thing, something that we still find ourselves doing but with sharper irony and self-consciousness – looking back on and in a sense living in carefully chosen periods and cultures, sometimes congenial to the point of escapism, sometimes exciting, mind-stretching, appalling. The novels of Walter Scott and Bulwer Lytton, Macaulay's *Lays of Ancient Rome*, transported vast numbers of enchanted readers into other times, other climes, where many found lifelong retreats, like cottages in the shires. Max maintained a home-from-home in the England of the Four Georges. G.K.C. discovered Dickens early and became and yet remains the all-time champion Dickensian. He could also enter imaginatively into the cottage economy of Cobbett's rural England or the life of guildsman or friar in the Middle Ages. Indeed, as T.S. Eliot is to observe, he could conjure the grand procession of Victorian worthies as a sort of Lord Mayor's Show.

We find them taking cognizance of the sweep of history, and their own chosen details within it, but like most of us they look out primarily upon their own age. But what was their "age"? We may find it at once too relaxing and too constricting to call "Edwardian." Queen Victoria has an Age, but she reigned sixty-four years (1837–1901); Edward VII reigned only nine years (1901–1910), but he had been for decades Prince of Wales, a man in the news, a world figure, as is proved by his being, by a wide margin, the favourite subject of Max for caricature. The Victorian Age had been on its way out for a long time, and the new time made latent questions patent – Samuel Butler is the quintessential Edwardian when he asks "what is 'art' that it should have a 'sake'"? Has science obviated religion somewhat or altogether? Is progress necessary? Mighty as the Empire is, should it be mightier yet? Insistent topics, for discussion, for obfuscation.

Bernard Shaw counted for both Max and G.K.C. Max succeeded him, and equaled him, as a weekly critic of drama and caught him, several times and for eternity, in caricature. G.K.C. encountered Shaw many times in widely publicised controversies, and his book about him established the importance of both. Of Shaw's more than ninety years the crucial decade is the Edwardian. Please allow King Edward his Age.

The vexatious question of "Modernity" arises for our two as for whom not? A brief answer is best. They lived in "modern" times. They joined no "modernist" movement. Max's earliest caricatures and writings were surprisingly new and well received, and he never thereafter fell from fashionable esteem into either oblivion or vulgar popularity. The captions of some of the prints, the allusions in some of the essays give them a suspicion of that "difficulty" that T.S. Eliot looked for in the modern as the "really new." Chesterton's earliest poems, *Greybeards at Play*, well received, were something new in satiric verse, and his earliest collection of essays, *The Defendant*, is serious and paradoxical in a modern mode, though the topos of the defence of the indefensible goes back to Antiquity.

Instead of venturing further into the marshlands of modernities, I raise the question of the "generation" in culture and literature as being much easier to handle and more useful. In any lifetime – in our own as experienced, in others' as observed or imagined – one is confronted by figures, a generation or less our senior, who are just in the process of achieving what you and I, their younger fellows, dream of attempting. Friend or rival, they serve as facilitator or blocker. Think of Ben Jonson coming to maturity in the shadow of Shakespeare. Think of

Pope and Dryden. Think of a young American approaching the Transatlantic Theme – vivid in his own experience, but vivid too in his current literary experience. "Look here, Strether, quit this." In apparent digression, actual simplification, I have devoted a chapter to a sort of ratio of generations: Max Beerbohm is to Walter Pater as G.K. Chesterton is to Oscar Wilde.

Further considerations of style and theme enter a somewhat miscellaneous chapter called "Turns on a Tandem." Surely a bizarre image – the new, Edwardian contrivance operated alternately by slim and dapper Max and bulky and rumpled G.K.C. Preposterous, but no more preposterous than the fact of their having any rapport or as their existing as they did in the first place. I can only hope that it will keep the reader in an indulgent mood.

Both were accomplished parodists, high among the best in the language, and both were caricaturists of vigour and inventiveness; true, and this deserves a chapter of its own. That leaves, at the end, "A Last Look."

WILLIAM BLISSETT
Toronto

in festo S. Georgii
A.D. MMXXI

CHAPTER ONE

First Acquaintance

It was Max Beerbohm, dapper, choosy Max – essayist, caricaturist, theatrical reviewer, and social success – who made the
first move. He was thirty, and the recipient of his letter, twen-
ty-eight:

4 May 1902   *Savile Club*

Dear Mr. Chesterton, I have seldom wished to meet anyone in particular: but you I should very much like to meet.

I need not explain who I am, for the name at the end
of this note is one which you have more than once admitted, rather sternly, into your writings.

By way of personal and private introduction, I may say
that my mother was a friend of your grandmother, Mrs
Grosjean, and also of your mother.

As I have said, I should like to meet you. On the other
hand, it is quite possible that *you* have no reciprocal anxiety
to meet *me*. In this case, nothing could be easier than for
you to say that you are very busy, or unwell, or going out of
town, and so are not able – much as you would have liked
– to lunch with me here either next Wednesday or next
Saturday at 1.30.

I am, whether you come or not, yours admiringly

MAX BEERBOHM

P.S. I am quite different from my writings (and so, I daresay, are you from yours). So that we should not necessarily fail to hit it off.

I, in the flesh, am modest, full of common sense, very genial, and rather dull.

What you are remains to be seen – or not to be seen by me, according to your decision.

Any answer to this note had better be directed to

48 Upper Berkeley Street, W.

for the porter of this club is very dilatory.

Before proceeding, may I explain Max's joke? "Modest!" The joke is that, some appearances to the contrary, Max really is modest, as all his friends will attest. "Dull!" The joke is that he is anything but, and whoever maintains that Max is dull must be himself a howling dullard. Observe also Max's assumption that, on the basis of their writings alone, they may fail to hit it off.[1]

The meeting took place and went well. Shall we surmise that it went like a house on fire? The simile has an obvious Chestertonian exuberance, but it was Max who so loved conflagrations that in flaming youth he denounced firefighters as "An Infamous Brigade" (1896) and returned to appreciate "The Fire" (1907) in its cosier and more life-enhancing aspects. Near the end of his life, in his *Autobiography* (1936), G.K.C. recalled the occasion with pleasure, with gusto. He begins by confirming Max's geniality and goes on to confirm his modesty:

About this time I discovered the secret of amiability in another person with a rather misleading reputation for acidity. [Other than Edmund Gosse, that is.] Mr. Max Beerbohm asked me to lunch; and I have ever since known that he is himself the most subtle of his paradoxes. A man with his reputation might well find offence in the phrase amiability; I can only explain to so scholarly a wit that I put it in Latin or French because I dare not put it in English. Max played in the masquerade of his time, which he has described so brilliantly; and he dressed or overdressed the part. His name was supposed to be a synonym for Impudence; for the undergraduate who exhibited the cheek of the guttersnipe in the garb of a dandy. He was supposed to blow his own trumpet with every flourish of self-praise; countless stories were told about the brazen placidity of his egoism.

Chesterton tells of two of these but notes that his friend's voice and the expression of his eyes refute such stories. Before he goes on, an error in orchestration must be corrected: surely it is their elder contemporary, Bernard Shaw, who blows a trumpet, Max's instrument being a woodwind. Chesterton continues:

> Most men spread themselves a little in conversation, and have their unreal victories and vanities; but he seems to me more moderate and realistic about himself than about anything else. He is more sceptical about everything than I am, by temper; but certainly he does not indulge in the base idolatry of believing in himself. On this point I wish I were as good a Christian as he. I hope, for the sake of his official or public personality, that he will manage to live down this last affront. But the people who could not see this fact, because an intelligent undergraduate enjoyed an intellectual rag, have something to learn about the possible combination of humility and humour.

This judgment is not simply a late afterthought on Chesterton's part: he had some time before, in an unpublished quatrain, jotted down his impression of his friend:

> And Max's queer crystalline sense
> Lit, like a sea beneath a sea.

Shines through a shameless impudence
As shameless a humility.[2]

Chesterton's judgment is a moral judgment, but he cannot deliver it without mentioning clothes. He sees Max as playing a part in "the masquerade of his time," as "dressed or over-dressed" in "the garb of a dandy." Thomas Carlyle had defined the dandy – and been quoted by Max – as a "clothes-wearing man," a definition that fits the Max of 1902 well enough, but "well enough" is not good enough for Max. Max was never quite that, never altogether in a state of art. True, he took a childlike pleasure in dressing up, primarily to please himself, to please everyone else incidentally. The Dandy (seldom met in his pure form) conveys an ideal self, an image of pulchritude and taste. Selfish? Immature? Perhaps, but there is always a residual, often a strong intention to convey delight, to confer a boon on the beholder. Max was a dandy in this generous sense; but what about Chesterton? He kept his big boy's love of swords and capes and the sweeping entrance and the big splash. Handsome as a youth and always impressive – no less than Max but how differently he conferred a boon by his presence, he cut a figure and was never quite altogether in a state of nature. It is not Chesterton but Father Brown who will be the ultimate anti-dandy. The little priest's presence and his actions always prove to be a blessing, but his appearance is never seen to confer a boon.[3]

Max and G.K.C. – to use the names that were becoming famous, like brand names for superior new products – found each other to be congenial opposites: concave and convex, slight and gigantic, slim and encompassing, reserved and exuberant, appraising and enthusiastic, tidy and untidy. Would it be too fanciful to relate them to Joyce's polarities of stem and stone – G.K.C. vast, luxuriant, forever branching out – Max concentrated, composed, "crystalline," in Chesterton's word, "impeccable," in the unfriendly word of Ezra Pound's Mauberley?[4]

It was, we have noted, the aloof, dandiacal Max who made the overture to the lunging, loose-fitting G.K.C. This is quite in Max's character. In a few years' time, though Arnold Bennett wrote the initial letter, it was Max who arranged the lunch. People did not "sit" to Max the caricaturist, but he generally needed to see them: as he said to Edmund Gosse, he brought "no pen, no notebook, merely a mild attentive gaze." To be sure, his first drawing of Chesterton was still two years in the future, and Max's motive was very probably to meet a fellow essayist; nevertheless, at any time G.K.C. must have been quite something to look at, and look at him he did, as his notes on the occasion prove:

> Enormous apparition. Head big for body – way of sinking head on chest. Like a mountain and a volcanic one – constant streams of talk flowing down – paradoxes flung up into the air – very magnificent.[5]

Gregarious Chesterton in contrast was easy enough to meet but seems not to have sought people out, rather to have welcomed whoever came his way with a Whitmanian embrace, as is shown in his invitation to "Humanity Esq, The Earth, Cosmos E – Mr. Gilbert Chesterton / requests the pleasure / Of humanity's company / to tea on Dec. 25th 1896." He omitted the RSVP. It is equally hard to imagine Max sending or acting on such an invitation, but he did recognize from the beginning the Chestertonian quality it embodies, for on 3 May 1902, the day before his letter, this passage appeared in his Saturday theatrical essay:

> A fashion paper for critics (why is there no such publication?) would tell us that the very latest mode is Optimism – Optimism in the very brightest colours and of the very amplest "make." This fashion for the coming Spring and Summer was set by (or, at least, finds its most ardent follow-

er in) Mr G.K. Chesterton, that excited and exciting novice, *quem honoris causa nomino.* At the cradle-side of that infant Hercules, current Life and Literature appear not as a pair of horrid snakes to be grappled with and strangled, but as two dear, kind, good snakes to be kissed, and to be romped with, and to have a lusty admiration lisped and crowed over them from the tips of their tails to the tips of their tongues.

His earliest caricature of his new friend will aim at catching this aspect of his personality – "Mr G.K. Chesterton giving the world a kiss" (1904).[6]

A brief pause, to consider the year 1902 more closely and to sound one sharp note of regret.

By the time of their meeting, Beerbohm and Chesterton were not exactly famous but were familiar figures in the London world of literary journalism. Max by that time has published *Works* (1896) and *More* (1898) and a set of caricatures. Since taking over from Shaw as dramatic critic for the *Saturday Review* he had written 53 articles before the meeting (of a final total of 466, by my count). G.K.C. by that time had brought out two books of mainly light and delightful poems and a collection of essays, *The Defendant*, employing the classical and Erasmian conceit of the defence of the indefensible, not to mention many as then uncollected articles. The two young writers, already "talked of," flourished in a year the chief event of which was the conclusion of the South African War. Max had nothing much to say about it, but G.K.C. had everything. Max must have known that he was making the acquaintance of an avowed and vocal Little Englander and anti-imperialist. In his last book, the *Autobiography* of 1936, Chesterton looking back came out and called himself not a pacifist or even a Little Englander but Pro-Boer.

In 1902, the first year of his reign, the new King Edward VII, pleased with Edward Elgar's music for the coronation, the *Pomp and Circumstance* marches, expressed the hope that one grand and stately march might be given words for a song. A respected figure, A.C. Benson, responded with the words "Land of Hope and Glory" and ending (twice) with "God, who made thee mighty / make thee mightier yet." Its success was prompt and lasting: it had been called a second national anthem.

If he had known his new friend longer, it would have been "Maximilian" for Max to have devised a definitive drawing – Chesterton in company with an assortment of Little Englanders trusting into song: "God, who made thee merry / make thee merrier yet."

Let us get to know the two of them as they were at the time of their meeting. In deference to his slight seniority of years and recognition, first Max. By this point, certainly, his special combination of talents was well defined. At school at Charterhouse he had already been known and admired and liked and probably a little feared for his drawings and satiric poems (in Latin). Already at Oxford he had achieved some distinction for the style of his pen and pencil in essay and caricature, for the style too of his clothes and conversation. The seven essays of his first collection were written mainly in his Oxford years (indeed, he remained an undergraduate, leaving the University without a degree, though under no cloud): this was the small, attractive book called, with impudence (G.K.C.'s word), *The Works of Max Beerbohm* (1896). It was supplied by its publisher, John Lane, with an accurate, mock-solemn bibliography. The last of these essays, "Diminuendo," ends thus:

> And I, who crave no knighthood, shall write no more. I shall write no more. Already I feel myself to be a trifle outmoded. I belong to the Beardsley period. Younger men, with months of activity before them, with fresher schemes and notions, with newer enthusiasms, have pressed forward since then. *Cedo junioribus.* Indeed, I stand aside with no regret. For to be outmoded is to be a classic, if one has written well. I have acceded to the hierarchy of good scribes and rather like my niche.[7]

Though craving no knighthood, he was to be knighted – forty years on. In spite of saying, twice, "I shall write no more," only three years later he brought out a new collection of twenty essays and called it, impudently, *More*. In 1896 he published *Caricatures of Twenty-five Gentlemen*. He had clearly made his mark in two arts, but that is not the same thing as making his fortune. He lived at home with his mother and sisters in Upper Berkeley Street and was much in demand socially, especially in those circles where his half-brother, Herbert Beerbohm Tree, the celebrated actor-manager, was a great lion. Max avoided subsumption into social success much as (*mutatis mutandis*) a later generation was to flee co-option into the Establishment: he could easily have been, could easily have cut, a merely fashionable figure. Max's play *A Social Success* (1913) presents an amiable young man who in desperation contrives to have himself caught cheating at cards in the vain hope of losing his place in society.[8]

In 1898 he succeeded Bernard Shaw as dramatic critic for the *Saturday Review*. Shaw recommended his successor to his readers with an echo, witty and incongruous, both of Max's own "Diminuendo" and of Ibsen's *Master Builder*, in a Max-like sentence ending in a carefully chosen and, as it proved, deathless epithet: "The younger generation is knocking at the door, and as I open it there steps sprightly in the incomparable Max." The incomparable Max: Max himself grew weary of the compliment, and in the Prefatory Letter to Bohun Lynch's book he adjures the author to "Compare me. Compare me as an essayist (for instance) with other essayists. Point out how much less human I am than Lamb, how much less intellectual than Hazlitt, and what an ignoramus beside Belloc; and how Chesterton's high spirits and abundance shame me...." From that I take heart in the present venture.[9]

Max supported himself by his weekly columns for twelve years, meeting Chesterton in the fourth of these. The theatrical reviews and essays have been collected in three sizeable volumes and are readable, and re-readable, but he found his weekly task irksome always and never acquired one scrap of professional facility. Nevertheless, he could maintain, early and late, that he never scamped his work. His friends should not have been so surprised when in 1910 he married, gave up theatrical reviewing, and left England to live the rest of his long life (except for war years and occasional visits) in Rapallo, a north-Italian coastal town, charming and blessedly cheap.[10]

Chesterton in contrast was a "sudden newcomer." The phrase is Max's, who will write: "in the year 1900 I had been considered a rather clever and amusing young man, but I felt no pang whatsoever at finding myself cut out at my own game by a sudden newcomer, named G.K. Chesterton, who was obviously far more amusing than I." (Is there a double edge to "obviously"?) Not really worried about his "game" himself, Max shows in his "Two Glimpses of Andrew Lang" (1928) just how worrying this sort of thing might have been. In the Nineties Andrew Lang had been an important and ubiquitous figure in the world of literary journalism and had been, along with Oscar Wilde, George Moore and George Meredith, the subject of one of Max's earliest literary caricatures. In his later years, Andrew Lang appeared in the *Illustrated London News* "week by week, in circumstances that touched sharply one's sense of pathos. Week by week, there was Chesterton rolling and rollicking up and down the columns of the front page, reeling off ideas good, bad, and indifferent – but always ideas, and plenty of 'em, and plenty more where they came from." And there too were Lang's essays at the back – "tired words ... about such trivial points in such tedious subjects of research." Max ruminates: "Would Chesterton some day fall back on such things? Once upon a time Lang had been alive and alert as Chesterton. A terrible thing, Time." He need not have worried: Chesterton (surely always more alive and alert than Lang) was not to outlive his alacrity of mind and his copious professional facility.[11]

The "game" Max refers to seems to be not simply the familiar essay in the then-thriving tradition of Lamb and Thackeray (and G.S. Street and E.V. Lucas, to name two almost forgotten contemporaries whom Max regarded as compeers) but more specifically the invention and projection of a distinctive and winning personality, or *persona*, so necessary if one is to survive and thrive in the literary market place. As he observed, "we live in an age of self-advertisement." In playing this game, he and G.K.C. (and some other vivid literary personalities, notably their friend Bernard Shaw) are following in the train of the first lord of language and publicity, Oscar Wilde. Ironically, the two contribute equally to an exaggerated picture of Wilde's Nineties that still persists, Max making the decade seem more sparkling and deft and stylish than any lump of temporal phenomena can ever have been, G.K.C. making it more decadent, pessimistic, or (to use the word he found particularly hair-raising) "impressionistic." Yes, impressionistic: for him, impressionism was "another name for that final scepticism that can find no floor to the universe" – surely one of the most melodramatic definitions ever offered of anything, even in the wild world of art criticism.[12]

They conspire, as it were, to solidify, to crystallize, the Nineties into something all too recognizable and intelligible. In fact, before coming to know him, Chesterton might well have thought of Max himself as somehow unwholesomely ninetyish, as resembling the famous drawing by Aubrey Beardsley – identified with Max – of a menacing foetus in evening clothes. This image of Max, as it happened, did not "take," nor did a more grateful one, just as ninetyish and mildly encouraged by one of his own self-sketches, of Max as Pierrot. Pierrot is a very fin-de-siècle figure, from Laforgue to Petrushka, and Max has the build for its costume but not its role: he is not stricken, macabre, pallid, not nocturnal or moonstruck, not pathetic or pining for love, not Franco-Italian in culture, and in half a lifetime "around theatres" he was always a spectator and never trod the boards.[13]

Max, putting Walter Pater in his place, said that he had not admired that stylist "even in the more decadent days of my childhood." G.K.C. recalls that preposterous phrase in writing of the "decadent days of my youth"; but he is serious, as is attested by his *Autobiography* and by his many biographers. The topic must not detain us here: suffice it to quote one passage from "Milton and Merry England" (1921):

> My first impulse to write, and almost my first impulse to think, was a revolt of disgust with the Decadents and the aesthetic pessimism of the 'nineties.' It is now almost impossible to bring home to anybody, even to myself, how final that *fin de siècle* seemed to be; not the end of the century but the end of the world. To a boy his first hatred is almost as immortal as his first love. He does not realise that the objects of either can alter; and I did not know that the twilight of the gods was only a mood. I thought that all the wit and wisdom in the world was banded together to slander and depress the world, and in becoming an optimist I had the feelings of an outlaw.

Finding Max to be, as man and artist, not tainted like the formal foetus, not even wan like the Pierrot of that decade-long minute, may perhaps more than anything else have induced Chesterton to phase out the note of melodrama in his subsequent references to the period. This question, present by implication in Max's initial letter, will keep recurring, and we shall need to take a close look at Max in relation to Pater, G.K.C. in relation to Wilde.[14]

At the point of their meeting, however, the Nineties are over, and G.K.C. is basking, Max chafing, in the bustle and welter of Edwardian Fleet Street, if not the high tide of human existence, surely the heyday of journalism, with its many and various newspapers and weeklies, not all of them as yet entirely corrupt. "I have always maintained," wrote Chesterton in 1909,

"quite seriously, that the Lord is not in the wind or thunder
of the waste, but if anywhere in the still small voice of Fleet
Street." He became a journalist in 1900 in order to marry and
was never to leave journalism even after he and Frances moved
from their Battersea flat (and he from the pubs of Fleet Street)
to the dormitory suburb of Beaconsfield in 1909, just the year
before Max turned his back forever on Fleet Street and settled
with his bride in Rapallo.[15]

After leaving St. Paul's School, Chesterton had been en-
rolled between 1893 and 1895 at the Slade School of Fine Art,
from which he received no diploma or certificate. Even after he
found himself as a writer, he continued off and on to exercise
a talent with pen, brush, and crayon. We shall have occasion to
consider some of his satiric drawings later. About this second
talent the doubly talented Max Beerbohm seems never to have
made a comment: for him, his friend is a writer, an essayist.[16]

Amusing himself, like Max, with the pretence that he was
much older than his years, G.K.C. had commenced to be an
author with the publication of an illustrated book of nonsense
verse, *Greybeards at Play* (1900). It attracted little attention in
its time but won high and deserved praise from W.H. Auden
and others. Almost concurrently he brought out a vigorous
book of serious verse, *The Wild Knight*. Thereafter, for all the
success of *The Ballad of the White Horse* (1911) and "Lepanto"
(1915), some jolly poems in praise of wine and an even jollier
one in dispraise of F.E. Smith, Lord Birkenhead (ending
"chuck it, Smith"), he is to be primarily a writer of prose. One
cannot say of him, as one is tempted to say (for effect) of Max,
that all his prose is better than any of his verse; but the verse of
neither will weigh much in our discussion.[17]

So thoroughly did Chesterton immerse himself in journalism and so highly applauded was the plunge that within a year
of the first two books of verse his first collection of essays, *The
Defendant* (1901), appeared, to be praised thus in the *Whitehall
Review*: "No one save Max Beerbohm has ever approached

these defences in whimsicality of idea and treatment." Max, for the *Yellow Book*, had written a "Defence of Cosmetics" (1894), later retitled "The Pervasion of Rouge" (scaring the timid with the accidental proximity of the word perversion). We may surmise that Chesterton on reading it had found his own vein and was away to the races, writing "Defences" of Penny Dreadfuls, Rash Vows, Skeletons, Publicity, Nonsense and eleven other oddly assorted things, including a "Defence of Humility" that begins in the true Chestertonian manner:

> The act of defending any one of the cardinal virtues has to-day all the exhilaration of a vice. Moral truisms have been so much disputed that they have begun to sparkle like so many brilliant paradoxes.

Rather re-invented than continued, first incidentally by Max, then in full amplification by G.K.C., the long tradition – rhetorical, sophistical, cynical – of the defence of the indefensible, the praise of the despicable, and close attention to the negligible, goes back to the Greeks, who gave us not only athletics but feats of agility with words and notions.[18]

This sort of thing measures itself against Oscar Wilde, of course, and against Max's first book, his most Wildean, as when, in comparing the late Victorian age with the Regency, he remarks, "We are not strong enough to be wicked, and the Nonconformist Conscience makes cowards of us all," or when in the essay on Cosmetics (which really did shock some readers – or at least some reviewers who felt it incumbent upon them to pretend to be shocked on their readers' behalf) he hails the end of the reign of terror of nature and rejoices now that "Artifice, that fair exile, has returned."[19]

At its most brilliant and characteristic, and at its most mature, Max's writing achieves surprise and point without paradox. This is true also of Wilde (less so of Chesterton), for in a review of *Earnest* (1909) Max takes note of "those merely verbal inversions which Oscar Wilde invented, and which in his day the critics solemnly believed – or at any rate solemnly declared – to be his only claim to the title of wit." No great wit uses only one device, and Wilde, Max says here and in his centennial tribute of 1954, was the wittiest talker he ever knew (Chesterton's name appears in the short list of others). Max is the master of the turn of phrase rather than the inverted truism; and of his carefully constructed phrases, in contrast to Wilde's, it may be observed that few if any of them could be taken up and turned into a slogan, a headline, or a quip. Wilde's disappointment with the Atlantic Ocean or his supposed statement to the New York customs, "I have nothing to declare but my genius," could be flashed round the world and lose nothing by being telegraphed. Max is just as witty and just as conceited but much less reportable when he writes, of the 1880s, "To give an accurate and exhaustive account of that period would need a far less brilliant pen than mine."[20]

Knowing as he did both Wilde and Chesterton (did anyone else so delight in, and so delight, both?), he was inoculated against their peculiarities of style. What he shared with both was a ready channel to the wellsprings of fun. How different, all three, from the acidic Whistler, not really laughing but uttering a harsh "ha!"; how different too from the unrejoicing poets of the nineties, be they aesthetic or hearty, be they Dowson, Kipling, Wratislaw, Henley, Yeats, Enoch Soames. What Max shared most especially with G.K.C. was a sense of style as an intuition of Being – not so much a boast of cleverness as it is a way of saying Glory to God for enabling a creature to display such dexterity. As stylists they are like those playful and social animals, the porpoise and the otter. The porpoise sports on the surface of great depths, the otter builds a playground in stream and pond. For their style of life they share the adverb *swimmingly*, in a sense not applicable to Pater or Wilde or even Shaw. The porpoise, as dolphin, is royal (like the eagle among birds and the lion among beasts), and there is something regal about Chesterton, like Old King Cole. The otter, like Max, belongs to the gentry and makes his playground for pleasure, unlike the workaday beaver for utility. The porpoise "blows" and breaks the surface with a great splash; the otter slips into the water with no splash at all, wonderful accomplishments, both.[21]

Having advanced this readily grasped and I hope amusing pair of images of visible sportiveness, I relinquish them: they will be teased no further.

Chesterton had already noticed Max in print ("rather sternly," we remember from Max's letter) before their first meeting. As early as January, 1902, he took note of "an airy and implied duel ... between Mr. Max Beerbohm, who defends the serious drama flippantly, and Mr. Clement Scott, who defends the flippant drama seriously.... Mr. Max Beerbohm, crowned with roses and with the epicurean wine-cup in his hand, calls all men to live a wild free life with him, watching the wreck of blameless families and the suicide of suburban pessimists. On the other hand, Mr. Clement Scott, pale with righteous indignation, swears by all the angels, by honour, by reverence, by the eternal moral instinct, that nothing shall separate him from Miss Ellaline Terriss and the great tradition of a fat man sitting down on his hat." In this "astonishing duel," the sympathy of the writer (I suspect), of the reader (I know), is with Max.[22]

The collection of biographical essays that anticipated his later literary biographies, *Twelve Types* (1902), makes no mention of Max, but in the expanded *Varied Types* (1903) he reaches back to include an essay on John Ruskin (1900) that praises the Victorian sage for his humour: "One tenth of his paradoxes would have made the fortune of a modern young man with gloves of an art yellow. He was as fond of nonsense as Mr. Max Beerbohm. Only ... he was fond of other things too. He did not ask humanity to dine on pickles." Perhaps Max in sending his invitation sought an opportunity to dissociate himself from pickles and to protest against the linking of his name with "art yellow" gloves, since as a freshman he had shuddered at his first sight of Walter Pater wearing gloves of bright dogskin. However, we know for a fact only that he and Chesterton talked of Browning at their first lunch and that Max, learning that G.K.C. had just been commissioned to write the study of Browning for the English Men of Letters series, said pensively, "a man ought to write on Browning while he is young." This seems a mock-serious remark, but four literary careers had begun with studies of Browning – Arthur Symons notably with his first book, Lionel Johnson, Owen Seaman the parodist and future editor of *Punch*, and Professor Walter Raleigh. As a matter of interest, in the book Browning is described as wearing lemon-coloured kid gloves.[23]

If *Robert Browning* (1903) is in some small measure a fruit of that conversation, the study of G.F. Watts, later that same year, opens with thoughts of the ups and downs of critical fashion and mentions Max by name. "The thing always happens sharply: a whisper runs through the salons, Mr Max Beerbohm waves a wand and a whole generation of great men and great achievement suddenly looks mildewed and unmeaning." Little did Chesterton foresee then that it would be Max's magic wand more than anything else that would bring Rossetti and his circle vividly to life, or that Max would recall meeting an old man who had seen as a boy "a gen'leman with summat long hair, settin' in a small cart, takin' a pictur'," and comment thus: "To me Ford Madox Brown's 'Work' is of all modern pictur's the most delightful in composition and strongest in conception, the most alive and the most worth-while." No mildew there. Max even wrote, though with reservations, about Watts:

> Many of the later Victorians had the advantage of G.F. Watts's fine and disinterested attention; but this advantage was not great. Watts himself, though in a way very different

from Maclise, was a light-weight; he was ethereal, and saw Browning and all those other massive persons of his day as spirits already in Heaven, at peace there, behind a golden haze which to-day gives one a sense of difficulty in finding one's way around the room devoted to them by the Trustees of the National Portrait Gallery.

Chesterton's somewhat laboured *Watts* finds its place between the vigorous *Browning* and the rip-snorting *Napoleon of Notting Hill*, just as the inadequate *Blake* stands between the spirited *George Bernard Shaw* and the earliest and best Father Brown stories. He is a literary man and a debater, and in writing about art he is writing with his left hand. The best thing in the *Watts* – and it is very good – is the essentially literary discussion of allegory and the reason that "in the whole range of Watts' symbolic art there is scarcely a single example of the ordinary and arbitrary current symbol, the ecclesiastical symbol, the heraldic symbol, the national symbol." The painter's object is "that the pictures may be intelligible if they survive the whole modern order," and this intelligibility remains ethical: it is unthinkable, G.K.C. argues (and here the sun comes out and beams) that Watts would paint "*The Victory of Joy over Morality*, or *Nature Rebuking Conscience*."[24]

Though never complete, the rapport of the two men was solidly based. They were both upper-middle-class Londoners, Max's father being "something in the city," the Chestertons being estate agents on a considerable scale in Kensington though G.K.C.'s father was not active in business. Their mothers could "know" one another. Never rich, they grew up in comfortable circumstances and on terms of easy familiarity with literature and the arts. They could have had entrée if they wished to Heartbreak House, but neither had any interest in or connection with Horseback Hall. The public personalities of the House of Commons were as familiar to either as the characters of Dickens and Thackeray, but neither was to be comfortable with the Whig oligarchs or neo-Tory imperialists. Both possessed a quality that linked them with the Victorians and with ordinary people and separated them from Ibsenism and Nietzscheanism and the "tragic generation" of the Nineties – and sundered them from the acridity and desperation of high modernism as it developed in their later years: they were cosy.[25]

Now to discriminate between them, in religion, in politics. Max's favourite sister, close to him in age and temperament, became an Anglican nun, but his own concern with religion remained slight, though as we shall see he could flare up with startling indignation at the "blasphemy" of Jerome K. Jerome's *Passing of the Third Floor Back*. The *fin-de-siècle* Catholicism of Oscar and Bosie and Aubrey was not for him, still less Chesterton's breezy undecadent religious stance. Surely one of the things that made G.K.C. so ill at ease about the decadent Nineties was campy Catholicism. Villiers de l'Isle-Adam, Verlaine, Huysmans in France, and then carrying on in England Beardsley, Wilde, Lionel Johnson, Ernest Dowson, even Canon John Gray and André Raffalovich, were not his galère, or Belloc's – but they were not really Max's set either.[26]

Again, G.K.C. remained a small-l liberal all his days, and Max a lower-case "tory anarchist." Compare their reactions to the death of Gladstone in 1898, the Grand Old Man, the embodiment of Liberalism at its egregious best. G.K.C. wrote a lachrymose poem, promptly published, Max made a set of scathingly unlachrymose drawings that were understandably long delayed in publication. The first of the eleven drawings shows the G.O.M. wearing down St. Peter, who has orders to exclude him, by threat of a prolonged peroration; in another, he addresses a mass meeting in Heaven and pays a graceful and eloquent tribute to God; and in a third, on leaving the meeting, Mr. Gladstone picks up a fallen angel. (Gladstone used to bring streetwalkers home to tea with Mrs. Gladstone, a virtuous, even heroically virtuous practice that lent itself to misconstruction.) Here, in sharpest contrast, rebuking the sort of young person Max wrote and drew for, are the concluding, stanzas of "To Them That Mourn":

> O young ones of a darker day,
>   In art's wan colours clad,
> Whose very love and hate are grey –
>   Whose very sin is sad,
>
> Pass on: one agony long-drawn
>   Was merrier than your mirth,
> When hand-in-hand came death and dawn,
>   And spring was on the earth.[27]

But here if they seem, and are, furthest apart, it should be recalled that Max's hardest-hitting caricatures, *The Second Childhood of John Bull* (drawn 1901, published 1911), coincide approximately in time and closely in spirit with G.K.C.'s bluntest and most unmirthful attacks on the triumphant juggernaut of imperialism. Neither man ever entertained an imperialist thought.[28]

CHAPTER TWO

The Reign of King Auberon

We must linger for a while in 1904, the most important year in our account. Then it was that Chesterton brought out his first work of extended fiction, The *Napoleon of Notting Hill*. Highly successful in its time, it was still remembered in 1948, when George Orwell wrote *Nineteen Eighty-Four*, and in 1984, when the action of their very different visions of the future takes place. It brings G.K.C. and Max together signally, since Auberon Quin, who at the outset of the tale is chosen by lot to be King of England, is the image of Max. In *Time Was*, a book of reminiscences that Max was to find delightful, the illustrator, W. Graham Robertson, recalls his commission in paragraphs that deserve extended quotation:

> Once, when I was particularly busy, arrived a bulky parcel containing a novel by G.K. Chesterton, which I regarded dubiously, wondering how I should find time to read it. But as I glanced at it, my eye fell upon the first phrase – "The Human Race, to which many of my readers belong" – and at once dispatched to Lane an enthusiastic recommendation. A book which begins like that must be all right; no one could afford to throw away such a gem in the opening sentence who had not plenty more to follow.[29]

He is not the first or the last to marvel at the copiousness of G.K.C.

A brief interruption to take in John Lane. At The Bodley Head he published many of the books we think of as setting the tone for the Nineties, including several illustrated by Beardsley, the *Yellow Book* and Oscar Wilde before his disgrace. In *The Importance of Being Earnest* Algy looks up from the piano and speaks the opening lines to his manservant – "Did you hear what I was playing, Lane?" – and Lane draws the first laugh with his reply – "I did not think it polite to listen, sir." Is Oscar, very gently, suggesting that there is something a bit servile and philistine about his publisher? Be that as it may, Lane has published Max up to this year, 1904, and here he is, one of the many publishers G.K.C. is keeping busy.[30]

Graham Robertson continues:

> I was enlisted to illustrate the work which turned out to be a witty and fantastic picture of a future England, reigned over by an elected King who appeared to be none other than Max Beerbohm, or at least a recognisable caricature of him. But Max, himself a caricaturist, was fair game; besides, he was in the secret and made no objections, and John Lane used to ask him and me to meet Mr. Chesterton, so that the collaboration between novelist, model and illustrator might become the more harmonious.

He goes on to allude to something that clearly rankles with him after many years. (His quotations from Chesterton are taken from a rather sour passage in the book on Bernard Shaw, 1910):

> Poor Max and I, in the freshness and innocence of our budding middle age, gambolled dutifully round the big man, all unconscious that – as he afterwards set down – he bracketed us together as interesting survivals of a bygone and evil period.

He found us, it seems, "most charming people" – always an ominous opening – and then went on to describe the type which, to him, we represented. It wasn't a very nice type. It had – "an artificial reticence of speech which waited till it could plant the perfect epigram." Now that couldn't have been I or I should have gone through life dumb. It was – "a cold, sarcastic dandy" – (a dandy! I, whose clothes always look like somebody else's misfits after I have worn them twice!) – "who went about with his one epigram, patient and poisonous, like a bee with its one sting." Now I'll take my oath that this wasn't Max: of all the witty men I have met he has the kindliest and most strictly disciplined tongue. Sometimes a hint of sly malice creeps into his caricatures, but there it is surely in its right place.

Really warming to his subject, Robertson concludes thus:

> I consider Max Beerbohm the perfect companion, because I always part from him with the impression that I, myself, have been brilliantly amusing. He is the most generous of wits; he not only casts his pearls before swine, but actually gives the swine the credit for their production.
>
> I regret that Mr. Chesterton did not appreciate us all the more because we both so thoroughly appreciated him.

It is as if in direct answer to this grievance, and to set right a record that he himself had set askew, that Chesterton in his last book, the *Autobiography* (1936), in recalling Max laid such great stress, as we have noted, on his amiability and his humility.[31]

By this account it appears that Robertson did not arbitrarily use Max's features in his illustrations but recognized Max in the character, and that G.K.C. and Max had both already assented to this. No fewer than five reviewers of the book when it appeared commented on the likeness to Max in Robertson's illustrations, which is unmistakeable, and on the identification of the character with Max, which is much more debatable. Frances Chesterton in her diary gives an account that meshes well, though not perfectly, with Robertson's:

> A delightful dinner party at the Lanes.... The talk was mostly about *Napoleon*. Max took me in to dinner and was really nice. He is a good fellow. His costume was extraordinary. Why should an evening waistcoat have four large white pearl buttons and why should he look that peculiar shape? He seems only pleased at the way he has been identified with King Auberon. "All right, my dear chap," he said to G., who was trying to apologize. "Mr. Lane and I settled it all at lunch." I think he was a little put out at finding no red carpet put down for his royal feet and we had quite a discussion as to whether he ought to precede me into the dining room. Graham Robertson was on my left. He was jolly too....[32]

Years later, in 1930, in a reminiscent mood, Chesterton wrote "A Note on Notting Hill," recalling an early essay by Max on "The Naming of Streets" (1902) and how it influenced the choice of venue of the novel:

> No person is, in the most serious sense, so wise and understanding as Mr Max Beerbohm. And I grieve to say that, in describing the effects of streets in altering his moods he wrote: "in Notting Hill High Street I become frankly common." Which is absurd; and impossible; and therefore quite uncommon. The fairies punished him by putting parts of him into my unfortunate story; along with an admirable portrait of him in Mr Graham Robertson's illustrations.

He is careful to dissociate himself from too great a particularity of locale:

But I confess that the original idea, in the conscious intellectual sense, was concerned with places like that in general; and my book might have been "The Washington of Walham Green" or "The Kosciuszko of Kensington Oval", or "The Garibaldi of Gunnersbury", or "The Charlemagne of Chiswick", instead of "The Napoleon of Notting Hill." For I have never been able to conceal entirely from a derisive world the fact that I was driving at something; though I had then got no further than asking in rather a wild way "Is there nothing that will save Notting Hill from being frankly common?"

The novel makes it all the more of a good joke nevertheless that the original of King Auberon should have confessed himself to feel "common," of all things, there, of all places. Besides, G.K.C. knew Notting Hill from boyhood days, as he could not have known most of the others.[33]

Max's essay is not perhaps quite so tangential to the novel as Chesterton's memory would make it. True, most of "The Naming of Streets" is occupied with anticipating a doctrine of Ferdinand Saussure, that tones of meaning are not inherent in words, witness the very different auras of Oxford and Oxford Street; but it begins by stating the issues, if not drawing the battle-lines, of *The Napoleon of Notting Hill*:

"The Rebuilding of London" proceeds ruthlessly apace. The humble old houses that dare not scrape the sky are being duly punished for their timidity. Down they come; and in their place are shot up new tenements, quick and high as rockets. And the little old streets, so narrow and exclusive, so shy and crooked – we are making examples of them, too. We lose our way in them, do we? – we whose time is money. Our omnibuses can't trundle through them, can't they? Very well, then. Down with them! We have no use for them. This is the age of "noble arteries."

Max goes on to observe, "There is but a tiny residue of persons who do not swell and sparkle. And of these glum by-standers at the carnival I am one." Chesterton had only to imagine Adam Wayne, and the conflict is joined. The indignant obstructor of such "noble arteries" is no glum bystander, but an activist who "swells and sparkles" indeed, but not with commercial avarice, rather with stern moral resolution, and declares in ringing words, "That which is large enough for the rich to covet ... is large enough for the poor to defend."[34]

Max Beerbohm is named in the book before Auberon Quin enters. Of the two young civil servants walking through London one wintry and dim morning it is said, "The lines of their frock-coats and silk hats had that luxuriant severity which makes the modern fop, hideous as he is, a favourite exercise of the modern draughtsman; that element which Mr. Max Beerbohm has admirably expressed in speaking of 'certain congruities of dark cloth and the rigid perfection of linen.'" The short young man who overtakes his taller friends with "imbecile cheerfulness" is introduced as Auberon Quin.[35]

We see Auberon first running to catch up with his friends: observe the lack of "side" in this. He is described:

> He had an appearance compounded of a baby and an owl. His round head, round eyes, seemed to have been designed by nature playfully with a pair of compasses. His flat dark hair and preposterously long frock-coat gave him something of the look of a child's "Noah". When he entered a room of strangers, they mistook him for a small boy, and wanted to take him on their knees, until he spoke ...

So far, almost a Max caricature of Max, but the sentence continues, snipping the bond of likeness, "... until he spoke, when they perceived that a boy would have been more intelligent." Now, it is true, these friends prove in the course of the narrative to be unreliable judges of intelligence, and Auberon will more than hold his own with them in his distinctive line of fantasy and nonsense. Nevertheless, not even the heartiest and least aesthetic of Max's acquaintances could ever have thought his conversation childish or have compared his room to an amethyst and himself to a turnip in it. It is as if G.K.C., just for a moment, had taken up Max's word in his letter – "rather dull" – only to drop it, permanently. I can account for it only as his signal to the reader not to make too much of the Beerbohm likeness – just as he is later to insist that Father Brown is clumsy, nondescript, and very English, to distance him from his model, that deft and distinguished Irishman, Father John O'Connor, with his "vocalic pulchritude."[36]

Max's gravitational field, however, though tiny, is powerful, and Auberon Quin soon takes on his elegance and aloofness, all turnips forgotten. Auberon's speech from the throne after having been chosen king by lot is pure Max, from its opening acceptance of advancing years. His Majesty explained that

> now old age was creeping upon him, he proposed to devote his remaining strength to bringing about a keener sense of local patriotism in the various municipalities of London. How few of them knew the legends of their own boroughs! How many there were who had never heard of the true origin of the Wink of Wandsworth! What a large proportion of the younger generation in Chelsea neglected to perform the old Chelsea Chuff! Pimlico no longer pumped the Pimlies. Battersea had forgotten the name of Blick.

He therefore imposes courtly ceremony and heraldic dress, entering himself fully into the glory of the mummery, the charade: "He wore an extravagantly long frock-coat, a pale-green waistcoat, a very full and *dégagé* black tie, and curious yellow gloves. This was his uniform as Colonel of a regiment of his own creation, the 1st Decadents Green." (Yellow gloves are back!)[37]

King Auberon's tone, as I hear it, owes much to G.K.C.'s "Defence of Heraldry" (1901), but something also to Max's most political essay, "If I Were Aedile" (1896) in *More*, a very civic-minded piece, grand, even regal in style, especially when he imagines himself addressing a delegation of developers. He begins:

> You are all of you very excellent, very ignorant, men. Meaning well in your scheme of "Betterment," you know nothing whatsoever about architecture. Style, character, beauty, tradition, are unintelligible to you. London is not a beautiful town, I know, but its aspect has fine qualities, to be revered. These qualities are the result of certain historical contrasts between the nobility, the burgesses, and the mob. You chafe at these contrasts....

And he ends: "I will answer no questions, hear no speeches. The deputation will now withdraw." Similarly, King Auberon: "The audience is at an end."[38]

Of all Chesterton's fictions, this one is the least concerned with religion. Its pageantry and mediaevalism are in no way ecclesiastical, its issues not overtly theological, and the small territory it so vividly evokes, open though it is to heaven, is a *polis* not a parish. Auberon's piety resides entirely in humour as a state of grace and in scruples of style. The foundation of Adam Wayne's conviction is in the Borough. The first meeting of the two protagonists is memorable. The newly chosen King feels himself poked in the ribs and regards through his single eye-glass (did Max, even in giddiest youth, ever sport a single eye-glass, as Thackeray did in giddy youth?) a boy with a wooden sword. "I'm the King of the Castle," says the boy, and Auberon replies, "I'm glad you are so stalwart a defender of your old inviolate Notting Hill. Look up nightly to that peak, my child, where it lifts itself among the stars so ancient, so lonely, so unutterably Notting...." It is then that perhaps the noblest of all his conceptions occurs to him – the thought of London suburbs vying and warring like arrogant mediaeval fiefdoms; and he gives the boy half a crown "for the war-chest of Notting Hill." The hill and its tower, first mentioned here, are to be crucial in the unfolding of the action; as is the boy.[39]

The boy, who is Adam Wayne, grows up to be a literalist of the imagination, Provost of Notting Hill, an immoveable object in the way of irresistible progress and development, in particular of one "noble artery" of commerce demanded by the other Boroughs. Auberon, hearing the grown-up Wayne's passionate defence, exclaims, "My God in Heaven! is it possible that there is within the four seas of Britain a man who takes Notting Hill seriously?" And Wayne's reply echoes the same words in the same order, with the addition of a ringing alliterative "not," so that the King can only remark weakly, "If this sort of thing is to go on, I shall begin to doubt the superiority of art to life." This sort of thing emphatically does go on, and becomes, Auberon realizes, "the one joke that may save me from pessimism," from the "hell of blank existence"; it may supply "a really entertaining miracle before I [go] to amuse the worms." Quin is, as Max would say, a "Tory anarchist," somewhat vitiated by aestheticism; Wayne is a fanatic, a militant, a crusader.[40]

Yes, a crusader, for the implicit Christianity of Wayne's stand makes itself manifest on one occasion, apropos of humour, when the King suggests that politics are "generally felt to be a little funny."

> "I suppose," said Adam, turning on him with a fierce suddenness – "I suppose you fancy crucifixion was a serious affair?"
>
> "Well, I –" began Auberon – "I admit I have generally thought it had its graver side."
>
> "Then you are wrong," said Wayne, with incredible violence. "Crucifixion is comic. It is exquisitely diverting. It was

an absurd and obscene kind of impaling reserved for people who were made to be laughed at – for slaves and provincials, for dentists and small tradesmen, as you would say. I have seen the grotesque gallows-shape, which the little Roman gutter-boys scribbled on walls as a vulgar joke, blazing on the pinnacles of the temples of the world."

Here Wayne and Auberon (and G.K.C. and Max) are poles apart; where they join is in their rejection of bureaucracy and Whiggery – Whiggery, that calm assumption that the world is best governed by a governing class, that those who have all the money and position and education should also have all the power.[41]

Once the conflict is joined and fun and games begin and blood flows in the streets, the outward action is pure Chesterton. King Auberon cannot save his realm from civil strife, but he certainly can write (almost like Max), and G.K.C. himself certainly can parody (again, almost like Max). Auberon not only writes lyrics about London under the pseudonym of Daisy Daydream but reviews them ferociously under the signature of Thunderbolt, including in his review *Hymns on the Hill*, another book of London poems, which is revealed to have been written in early youth by none other than Adam Wayne. Both poets had praised the hansom cab. Daisy:

> Poet, whose cunning carved this amorous shell,
> Where twain may dwell;

and Wayne:

> The wind round the old street corner
> swung sudden and quick as a cab;

and Thunderbolt:

"Daisy Daydream" thinks it a great compliment to a hansom cab to be compared to one of the spiral chambers of the sea. And the author of "Hymns on the Hill" thinks it a great compliment to the immortal whirlwind to be compared to a hackney coach. He surely is the real admirer of London. We have no space to speak of all his perfect applications of the idea; of the poem in which, for instance, a lady's eyes are compared, not to stars, but to two perfect street-lamps guiding the wanderer. We have no space to speak of the fine lyric, recalling the Elizabethan spirit, in which the poet, instead of saying that the rose and lily contend in her complexion, says, with a purer modernism, that the red omnibus of Hammersmith and the white omnibus of Fulham fight there for the mastery. How perfect the image of two contending omnibuses!

Two harassed journalists, G.K.C. as writer of the ensuing sentence and Max as reader, must have smiled rather ruefully: "Here, somewhat abruptly, the review concluded, probably because the King had to send off his copy at that moment, as he was in some want of money."[42]

Just as amusing as this parody of literary reviewing is the parody of war journalism when King Auberon is accredited as a special correspondent and sends in a succession of heavily erased paragraphs, having attempted several styles:

At the side of one experiment was written, "Try American style" and the fragment began –

"The King must go. We want gritty men. Flapdoodle is all very ...;" and then broke off [how one wishes James Joyce had laid off the American slang in "Oxen of the Sun" so promptly], followed by the note, "Good sound journalism safer. Try it."

The experiment in good sound journalism appeared to begin – "The greatest of English poets has said that a rose by any ..." This [shall we call it an exercise by T. Fenning Dodworth?] also stopped abruptly.

The next, and longest, attempt is in an elaborate, enamelled, carefully honed aesthetic style. After describing, with lingering appreciation, the leaders of the converging forces and their heraldic colours, it concludes thus:

> The whole resembles some ancient and dainty Dutch flower bed. Along the crest of Campden Hill lie the golden crocuses of West Kensington. They are, as it were, the first fiery fringe of the whole. Northward lies our hyacinth Barker, with all his blue hyacinths. Round to the south-west run the green rushes of Wilson of Bayswater, and a line of violet irises (aptly symbolized by Mr. Buck) complete the whole. The argent exterior ... (I am losing the style. I should have said "Curving with a whisk" instead of merely "Curving." Also I should have called the hyacinths "sudden." I cannot keep this up. War is too rapid for this style of writing. Please ask office-boy to insert the *mots justes*.)

"Dainty" is a favourite word of Walter Pater, who can refer to clouds as "sudden."[43]

Part of the effect of "fairy tale" in Notting Hill is inherent in what passes for prosaic – red goblin pillar-boxes, the green omnibus as enchanted ship; part depends on the embellishment of the prosaic by a lively romantic and heraldic fantasy. As late as 1930, recalling *The Napoleon of Notting Hill*, G.K.C. wrote: "I still hold ... that the suburbs ought to be either glorified by romance and religion or else destroyed by fire from heaven, or even by firebrands from the earth." While events are stationary, in siege, "the very prose of warfare," G.K.C. can indulge an almost Maximilian taste for parody, but soon battle, bloodshed, exhilaration, take over, culminating in the famous victory of the water-tower, and leading eventually to the imperialist hegemony of Notting Hill over the defeated boroughs and their overthrow of the victor in turn.

At the end of the story, when Adam Wayne and Auberon Quin, the pure fanatic and the pure satirist as they are called, go forth together – into eternity, it seems – it is no longer two characters, one of them Max, who go, but two aspects of Chesterton's personality, two thin men within his ample frame. Max here can "step sprightly in," for a time, but in the later fiction of G.K.C. there will be no place for the likes of Max.[44]

CHAPTER THREE

Old Times and New

Max really did like *The Napoleon of Notting Hill* and was not just going affably along with the joke. He cannot have been intellectually vanquished by it, for in the very first of the hundreds of weekly pieces G.K.C. wrote for the *Illustrated London News* (30 September 1905), he confessed himself "deeply grieved to see that Mr. Max Beerbohm has been saying that he does not find London beautiful or romantic." "Has been saying": the tense implies an opinion not fixed in the past of "If I were Aedile" (1896) or "The Naming of Streets" (1902) but continuing in the post-Napoleonic present. Be that as it may, writing to Reggie Turner, Max says, "I think it awfully good. I wonder if you will relent about the author. You told me he lacked "heart." I think there is plenty of that organ mixed up in the book." This is to be the tone of most of the further references to Chesterton.[45]

Not all. Max was always candid in writing to Reggie, his friend from Oxford days. On a later occasion (1910) he wrote: "I thought G.K.C.'s *What's Wrong with the World?* very cheap and sloppy, though with gleams – gleams of gas-lamps in Fleet Street mud and slush" – the Fleet Street whose mud and slush he had in that year finally scraped from his shoes. In the following year he added that "Chesterton doesn't wear well at all, though I'm not sure whether it is that he has lost his quality or merely that he hasn't acquired a new quality to keep me interested." Chesterton himself was uneasy about the title of the book, which was not exactly what he had intended, and perhaps a little embarrassed about the whole performance: in his dedication to C.F.G. Masterman he said, "as far as literature goes, this book is what is wrong, and no mistake," and later on he calls it "this crude study." Here if anywhere he adopts not just the stance of the controversialist but the tone of "thou fool." At some point in his leisurely life Max took pains to decorate the title page of his copy – a besmattered title page, or is it merely foxed? – G.K.C.'s visage looks belligerent as well as bloated, and his teeth spell "seventh edition." There is a letter of 1924, apparently to Will Rothenstein, in which Max says, "No, I am not nearly so witty as Chesterton for one. But certainly I have not prostituted and cheapened my wit as he has."[46]

It is comforting to be able to report that the friendship did not come to an end. A small indication of renewed liking occurs in a letter to A.B. Walkley (1922): "I think I twitted you, last Spring, apropos of an account you gave me of your having sat between Chesterton and Belloc at some dinner, with being over-hard to please about people whom you weren't, after all, destined to spend the whole of your life with. Heaven forbid that C. and B. should *forever* flank you!" Later, in 1935, Max and Florence rejoiced at the visit of Gilbert and Frances to Rapallo – "enormous as compared with what he was; but delightful." In expressing his own pleasure at hearing G.B.S. and G.K.C. on the radio that Reggie Turner had given him, he assumes that Reggie will share his good opinion:

> G.B.S.'s acting quite capital. But he's no good in a "talk": much too loud and quick – too platformy and grimly determined to be a vigorous hefty youth. G.K. Chesterton *very* good, don't you think? The right technique. A friend in one's room, pensively and quietly monologising.

(The very qualities Max himself is to cultivate and achieve in his radio talks.) Only a year later, Max stood at the graveside of

Chesterton. This act of piety pretty well concludes the account of Max's comments on his friend, with the great exceptions of the parody in *A Christmas Garland* and the caricatures, which I have reserved to the end.[47]

Max's output is manageable in size and accessible in great part to any interested reader. There is, in contrast, such profusion and plenty in Chesterton that his casual readers feel free to pocket windfalls, but literary historians are obliged to pick up after him. That is what I intend to do now with the rather bulky remainder of his mentions of Max and the places in his writings where he may have had Max in mind or we in our special context are likely to recall him. The result may be a bit miscellaneous, but, hang it, Chesterton is miscellaneous or he is nothing. No chronological unfolding of interest is discernible. Instead, I offer a roughly fivefold consideration. In the first section, G.K.C. is as it were looking back with Max at earlier periods in which they both took an interest, especially the Regency and the Victorian Age, and looking out with Max on modern times. Then the promised treatment of Pater and Wilde. These rather long sections are followed by a short one in which G.K.C. looks at Max's caricatures. Then, for the record, but also I think for their inherent interest, we shall observe instances of G.K.C. casually reading or remembering other passages in Max's writings; and finally, instances of G.K.C. evidently reading Max with critical attention. Then a return to Max, to parody, to caricature.

Chesterton had the Middle Ages to himself, Max's Horatian Latinity being perhaps the equivalent of G.K.C.'s mediaevalism. Chesterton boldly and successfully entered the world of St. Francis and St. Thomas Aquinas, and less happily that of Chaucer, but Max never ventured as his hero Rossetti did into the circle of Dante or the Camelot of King Arthur. Like Benjamin Jowett in his drawing, Max might ask what they were going to *do* with the Holy Grail when they found it? As he observes at the beginning of "Enoch Soames," the holy grail for his generation was the *mot juste*. The Beardsley Period has succeeded the age of Burne-Jones.[48]

The earliest period at which they will both look back is the late 18th century. Chesterton, who resembled a toby-jug of Dr. Johnson, wrote and acted in a lively play, *The Judgement of Dr. Johnson* (1927), and Max in his vintage essay, "A Clergyman" (1918), takes an unemphatic moment in Boswell and brings out all its capabilities. Chesterton so thought of Max as belonging to the eighteenth century that he protested against his growing a moustache as out of historical character.[49]

Nevertheless, it is safe to say that, for both, real life and modern times and English literary history begin at the Regency – that "quaint period, (beloved of Mr. Max Beerbohm)" as G.K.C. puts it. As early as 1894 (the year before *The Importance of Being Earnest*) Max, in the "spirit of real earnestness" (that is, with more than usual irony and playfulness compounded with, spiced with, seriousness) had praised the Prince Regent's services to style and *ton* and artifice and gaiety and tried to bind up the wounds inflicted on him by the usually gentle Thackeray in *The Four Georges*. Chesterton in the early *Varied Types* (1903), in assessing Charles II as, unlike George IV, "a rascal, but not a snob," is quoting Thackeray, and in another essay he speaks of Wellington's "strange humility which made it physically possible for him without a gleam of humour or discomfort to go on his knees to a preposterous bounder like George IV." Something made him change his mind later; and perhaps Max contributed. G.K.C.'s preface to the annual *Essays by Divers Hands* of the Royal Society of Literature (1926) deals in part with George IV, who had been the first to encourage the Society – "a man who had the makings of a very fine, because a very free, patron of letters; for in his youth he loved not only literature, but liberty," but was broken and died as a man when he became king. Though he says nothing about clothes and little about style, Chesterton in asserting the moral worth of the man is closer to Max now than to Thackeray. In the same year he reviewed Shane Leslie's *George IV*, which he terms not a "whitewash" but the "restoration of a blackened picture" and concludes that "the friend of Fox and Sheridan cannot possibly have been a mere dummy dressed up as a dandy; and that the man whom Canning and Castlereagh often thought too clever for them can hardly have been entirely a fool.[50]

Max's *Happy Hypocrite* (1897), which can pass as a children's book, is set in the Regency and has as its hero Lord George Hell (George: the same name as the Prince Regent and Beau Brummell). Though patterned in style on the fairy tales of Oscar Wilde, it tells the triumph of love and humility over a proud self-sufficiency, and so obeys *ex animo* the "ethics of elf land" that Chesterton is to expound in *Orthodoxy*. Chesterton's own essay on the great Regency town of Bath (1925) is appreciative enough, though not particularly high-spirited. It praises Beau Nash for his order that no swords be worn in Bath, which is more in keeping with Max's pacific nature than with his own comically bellicose love of swords and swordsticks. He adds that such measures seem not to have reduced the amount of violence in the world; highly debatable. One other, rather surprising link with the Regency is seen when he takes issue with Max by recalling that Thackeray's father, very much a man of that period, had with a chuckle recommended that the boy read Tobias Smollett's *Peregrine Pickle*, that rowdy and unimproving novel: "Even a modern so steeped in the eighteenth century as Mr. Max Beerbohm has described the typical papa of a generation that might well have been that of Thackeray's papa, as a gloomy and ponderous person who talked to his children about nothing but Hell." I have not located the passage referred to, but it sounds more like a quip on Max's part than a settled opinion.[51]

Within the Victorian Age it was the 1880s that occasioned one of Max's most Maximilian sentences, the mild disclaimer, already quoted, that "to give an accurate and exhaustive account of that period would need a far less brilliant pen than mine."

True, he could never have allowed himself the ample scope of Chesterton's two books on Dickens or his *Victorian Age in Literature*, in the latter of which especially G.K.C.'s pen was quite brilliant enough to prompt his pusillanimous publisher to issue a cowering disclaimer. Nevertheless, by implication the deft drawings and their often full and always amusing captions in *Rossetti and his Circle* comprise an excellent and indispensable critical and historical comment on the later Victorian decades. Independently conceived, the two are remarkably congruous, as in (to take only one example) their treatment of John Stuart Mill, the saint of Utilitarianism. Here is Chesterton:

> Though he had to preach a hard rationalism in religion, a hard competition in economics, a hard egoism in ethics, his own soul had all that silvery sensitiveness that can be seen in his fine portrait by Watts. He boasted none of that brutal optimism with which his friends and followers of the Manchester School expounded their cheery negations. There was about Mill even a sort of embarrassment; he exhibited all the wheels of his iron universe rather reluctantly, like a gentleman in trade showing ladies over his factory. There shone in him a beautiful reverence for women, which is all the more touching because, in his department, as it were, he could only offer them so dry a gift as the Victorian Parliamentary Franchise.

Max's drawing shows Mill, top hat in one hand, briefcase in the other, gaunt and (on second look) sensitive and (yes, on third look) silvery. John Morley, a forceful figure in both politics and letters, is introducing his friend, at considerable length, to a pensive and noncommittal Rossetti:

> "It has recently," he says, "occurred to Mr. Mill that in his lifelong endeavour to catch and keep the ear of the nation he has been hampered by a certain deficiency in – well, in

warmth, in colour, in rich charm. I have told him that this deficiency (I do not regard it as a defect) might possibly be remedied by *you*. Mr. Mill has in the press at this moment a new work, entitled 'The Subjection of Women.' From my slight acquaintance with you, and from all that I have seen and heard of your work, I gather that Women greatly interest you, and I have no doubt that you are incensed at their subjection. Mr. Mill has brought his proof-sheets with him. He will read them to you. I believe, and he takes my word for it, that a series of illustrative paintings by you would" etc., etc.

On the wall behind them is a painting of a woman, a "stunner" in the best Rossetti mode, in no way deficient in warmth, in colour, in rich charm. In his early book on Browning G.K.C. had observed, with something like a wink, that "women in Rossetti's pictures did not look useful or industrious" also that "the man who objects to the Rossetti pictures because they depict a sad and sensuous day-dream, objects to their existing at all." We must not leave John Stuart Mill without mention of the very earliest relevant object to be found: E.C. Bentley in 1893 had just invented the clerihew; here is the one on Mill, illustrated by the youthful G.K.C.

John Stuart Mill,
By a mighty effort of will,
Overcame his natural bonhomie
And wrote *Principles of Political Economy.*
  "– With some of their Applications to Social Philosophy."[52]

Like Max, Chesterton met Swinburne, though only once, "upon a sort of privileged embassy; and such impressions may easily be illusions." When, severally, they encountered this legendary incarnation of genius, youth, passion, and revolt, it was late in the poet's life, and he was, in G.K.C.'s words, a sort of god in a temple, who could only be approached through a high priest. I had a long conversation with Watts-Dunton and then a short conversation with Swinburne. Swinburne was quite gay and skittish, though in a manner that affected me strangely as spinsterish; but he had charming manners and especially the courtesy of consistent cheerfulness. But Watts-Dunton, it must be admitted, was very serious indeed. It is said that he made the poet a religion; but what struck me as odd, even at the time, was that his religion seemed to consist largely of preserving and protecting the poet's irreligion. He thought it essential that no great man should be contaminated with Christianity.

This brief account concludes with a vigorous restatement of the argument that Swinburne's pantheism is incompatible with his revolutionary fervour. The contrast with Max's celebrated account of his visits to "Number 2, The Pines" in 1899 is instructive, but it would be unfair to compare G.K.C.'s brief passage with this masterpiece. Compare it rather with Max's vivid, breathless notes jotted down immediately after a visit:

The romance of seeing him – Luncheon on table – door opened – Little gray figure – huge dome of head – pale – revolving eye – stomach – pink nose – slippers – But "And did you once see Shelley plain? And did you speak with him again?" Old-fashioned – aristocratic – bow from the waist – Deafness cutting him away – Tremulous hand – painful longing at a pint of Bass – [....] Always same procedure – (boiled mutton and caper sauce – apple tart – cheese – Both at dinner and luncheon) Theodore not so deaf – Monopolizing – Then a shout – Give me his head – Lyric outpour – Rhapsodies – sing-song – effeminate – babyish [....] Intoxication – saturation – fusty, musty – Go out into the street – sunshine, or gas-lamps – Vulgarity – Certain horror – yet relief.

Max's whole desire is to catch Swinburne at home, Chesterton's to catch him out.[53]

The years from 1885 to 1898, called by Max the "Beardsley Period," were for Chesterton "like the hours of afternoon in a rich house with large rooms; the hours before tea-time. They believed in nothing except good manners; and the essence of good manners is to conceal a yawn. A yawn may be defined as a silent yell." The young pessimist of the time "yawned so wide as to swallow the world." In these good phrases, and in the Dedicatory poem (to E.C. Bentley) of *The Man Who Was Thursday*, G.K.C. conveys some of the sense of moral danger involved in being intelligent and young in the Nineties, but when he tries to embody such characters in fiction, they make too much noise, create too big a splash, like the ardent but futile genuine anarchist in *Thursday* or the sinister Islamic infiltrator, Lord Ivywood, in *The Flying Inn*. He could never have created Enoch Soames, the quintessential decadent poet of Max's *Seven Men*, who sells his soul to the Devil for the fruition of posthumous fame. I am afraid he would have come down hard on poor Enoch and missed some of the absurdity and most of the pathos – a pathos Max himself was late to appreciate. The last, and least, of Chesterton's melodramatizations of the Nineties is the observation that Robert Louis Stevenson escaped as from a city of the dead the world of Enoch Soames.[54]

Pater, Beardsley, Wilde – three key figures of the decade, who died in 1894, 1898, 1900. Two of them, Pater and Wilde, we shall soon be discussing at some length. Chesterton in a youth he once called decadent must have needed to resist the third, Aubrey Beardsley: we know that he kept a notebook full of horrifying and grotesque drawings. In the drawings we have, however, there is nothing suggestive, nothing creepy. One of the funniest sentences in his high-spirited romance, *The Flying Inn* (1914), is this: "Lady Enid Wimpole still overwhelmed her earnest and timid face with a tremendous costume, that was more like a procession than a dress. It looked rather like the funeral procession of Aubrey Beardsley." Max, who was an exact contemporary of Aubrey, and knew him, and felt the anguish of his untimely death, could never have written so. Chesterton at this moment seems a whole generation removed, not just two years younger.[55]

Departure in 1908 and 1910 to Beaconsfield and Rapallo seems to have ended any close interest or engagement with the newer developments in literature on the part of our two writers. Interest in Bernard Shaw was lifelong with both – but in how few others. True, Max will continue to read Henry James and Joseph Conrad, who belong to modernity if not to modernism, and G.K.C. can even mention Ezra Pound and Wyndham Lewis, Eric Gill and T.S. Eliot, about whom one might expect him to be perfectly blank. The Great War is, of course, a primary cause of cultural discontinuity; but well before its outbreak they had both found out what they had to do and were doing it without regard to the Modern Movement. Max might plead that he had done his duty by modernism when a dramatic critic: the dramatist Maurice Maeterlinck received from him more consistently admiring mentions and reviews than any other playwright living or dead and Maeterlinck was a symbolist or he was nothing. And G.K.C. might plead that he was always and forever discovering and displaying the newness of Christianity and the mouldiness of its successive rivals. Still, T.S. Eliot compared Chesterton to a cabman thumping himself to keep warm; and Max, who could see nothing in Proust or Joyce, could see everything, and more, in Lytton Strachey.[56]

CHAPTER FOUR

The Man Pater and the Man Wilde

Here begins a long digression, or excursus, based less on simple comparison than on a ratio: Max Beerbohm is to Walter Pater as G.K. Chesterton is to Oscar Wilde. It is a ratio that requires a little initial subtraction. Max and Pater were both stylists, but Pater holds a place in the history of ideas that Max cannot challenge. G.K.C. and Wilde were both paradoxical moralists, very much in the public eye, but Oscar can apply himself to his art with an earnestness that the other reserved for religion. All four were highly literary and project literary personalities recognizable on just about every page.[57]

A certain deficiency or absence shared by all four may be noted at the outset. In this they are joined by Mr. Salteena in Daisy Ashford's *The Young Visiters*, who "Asked a few riddles as he was not musicle." None was musical at the dawn of an age dominated by literary musicality – inspired, ironically, by Pater's famous dictum that all art constantly aspires towards the condition of music. One thinks at once of Joyce and Proust and Thomas Mann, of Mallarmé and Valéry and Eliot, even of George Moore and Aubrey Beardsley. But Pater's own art conspicuously does not so aspire. This is not simply because he neglects the appreciation of music and musicians while cultivating that of the visual and literary arts. His writing is marked, to be sure, by the recurrence of certain words that might be taken for signature themes or leitmotifs, and, as we shall be noticing, his initial "Well!" rings out like Wilde's terminal "That is all." But in two carefully considered passages the word he chooses to characterize music is "vague" – something no musician, not even Debussy, not even Delius, would countenance. Edward Thomas's ear is true when he notices Pater's repetitions, "so that one page contains '*finesse*,' 'nicety' twice, 'daintiness,' 'light aerial delicacy,' 'simple elegance,' 'gracious,' 'graceful and refined,' and 'fair, priestly'; they continually remind us of the author's delight in delicacy, elegance, etc., and his always obviously conscious use of language does the same." But, he continues, all this is non-auditory: "His very words are to be seen, not read aloud; for if read aloud they betray their artificiality by a lack of natural expressive rhythm." Later, after excepting the famous passage on La Gioconda from his strictures, he makes the same point again, enlisting Oscar Wilde in his support. The passage he quotes demands quotation here:

> Since the introduction of printing, and the fatal development of the habit of reading among the middle and lower classes of this country, there has been a tendency in literature to appeal more to the eye, and less and less to the ear which is really the sense which, from the standpoint of pure art, it should seek to please, and by whose canons of pleasure it should abide always. Even the work of Mr. Pater, who is, on the whole, the most perfect master of English now creating among us, is often far more like a piece of mosaic than a passage in music, and seems here and there to lack the true rhythmical life of words and the fine freedom and richness of effect that such rhythmical life produces.

Wilde's word "mosaic" is better than A.C Benson's "opal," since we know that Pater's method of composition was to spread out slips of paper with single sentences written on them and arrange them in sequence – the method of Bacon's early essays and the furthest remove from musical composition.[58]

The other three are gifted conversationalists, Wilde especially being in conversation and story-telling the equivalent of a *bel-canto* tenor of the first order, and their writing sounds better read aloud than Pater's does, but that is not sufficient to make them musical. Oscar Wilde talked well about everything in the world of talk, including musical events, and frequented the opera – for the conversation; but when one of his wits offers to play "some mad scarlet thing by Dvořák," he seems unaware that the only mad scarlet thing about that composer is the spelling of his name. If he had lived to hear Strauss's *Salome*, he would doubtless have applauded, but that is neither here nor there. As for Max, he was an inveterate play-goer before he became a professional one, but never a concert-goer. In his essay, "At Covent Garden," Max confesses: "I am quite indifferent to serious music, and I should not suffer from any sense of loss if all the scores of all the operas that have ever been written, and all the persons who might be able to reconstruct them from memory, were to perish in a sudden holocaust tomorrow." I have found no mention of his having attended any of the concerts featuring early and modern music organized by Ezra Pound in Rapallo, though they were of high musical interest and must have been the most notable cultural events in Liguria in the 1930s. I do not believe that he, or anyone, would adduce his lifelong love of the music hall as evidence of musical interest or taste. Chesterton when most strongly under the influence of Belloc wrote a number of songs that certainly can be recited with gusto, so *why* shouldn't they be sung, or roared? These are the verses in *The Flying Inn*, separately collected as *Wine, Water and Song*. But it is surely significant that the most vigorous and various Christian apologist of the past century should never, in his myriads of writings (tell me if I have missed one) – should never have noticed that Christianity is, among the religions of the world, the musical religion. I am thinking not so much of the great church composers – Palestrina and Byrd, Bach and Handel, Franck and Bruckner, Willan and Messiaen – as of the great chants and hymns known to the millions but not, it seems, to Chesterton. (He did write a hymn, still sung, which contains the unfortunate plea, obtrusively clever, "from sleep and from damnation, deliver us, O Lord"). Perhaps, like his great enemy, Dean Inge, he did not see the necessity for a perpetual serenading of God. Music was, the least of his interests, and it was not very much more than that for the other three.[59]

In both pairs the younger rejects the elder, not simply as an external force in the world of literature and ideas nor yet as anything so intimate as a father figure, but rather as a lost leader, a disappointing or errant uncle. There is evidence in both cases of deep engagement, decision, rejection. I begin with Max and Pater.

A reader in 1896, opening *The Works of Max Beerbohm*, would find an epigraph, in quotation marks but unidentified, carefully set in a typography of diminuendo:

> "Amid all he has already here achieved, full, we may
> think, of the quiet assurance of what is to come,
> his attitude is still that of the scholar; he
> seems still to be saying, before all
> things, from first to last, 'I
> am utterly purposed
> that I will not
> offend.'"

One of the few commentators to notice this, in parenthesis, remarks: "That, from the epigraph to his first and most aggressively self-advertising book, turns out to be more an ironic warning than an apology. It is the good intention of the habitual offender."[60]

It would be well to identify the source of the quotation. It is by Pater, the concluding sentence of an essay on Raphael delivered as a lecture at Oxford in August, 1892, and published in the *Fortnightly Review* in October; it was collected after Pater's death (30 July 1894) in *Miscellaneous Studies* (1895). Max of course was an undergraduate at Merton in 1892, but August is out of term (and an off-time for a university occasion, surely), and Max's father died at the end of August, and so it is almost certain that he was not present at the lecture – especially since he found Pater inaudible, but there must have been something in the printed essay that caught his eye. What? "From first to last" is a phrase we shall find applicable both to Pater's essay and to Max's book.

Pater's essay begins: "By his immense productiveness, by the even perfection of what he produced, its fitness to its own day, its hold on posterity, in the suavity of his life, some would add in the 'opportunity' of his early death, Raphael may seem a signal instance of the luckiness, of the good fortune, of genius." A young man of genius, reading such a sentence, might well suspect Pater of considering the early death of any young man of genius "opportune," though Max, at twenty-three, a few pages later could take comfort at the news that Raphael did not die until he was thirty-seven. Well! (as Pater himself says, warming to his subject): "The scrupulous scholar, aged twenty-three, is now indeed a master; but still goes carefully. Note, therefore, how much more exclusion counts for in the positive effect of his work." This fits Max to perfection. And it leads very soon to the concluding sentence of the essay, chosen by Max as his epigraph.

What exactly is it "not to offend"? There must be nothing unskillful, uncouth, gawky, hobbledehoy; nothing shrill or booming, too slow or too loud. It can of course take the sense of "not to fall into sin," but Pater's context does not encourage it and Max's precludes it: rather, Max belongs among those "gentlemen" defined by Oscar Wilde as "never giving offence unintentionally." We are alerted to the possibility of some covert aggression and recall the anxious question of an uncle-father – "Is there no offence in it?" and Hamlet's reply, "They do but jest, poison in jest, no offence in the world."

If Max's *Works* open with this polite and seemingly inoffensive epigraph, derived as it happens from Pater, it ends with the essay "Diminuendo," in which Pater himself has a walk-on part. This essay was written in Chicago in the summer of 1895 and may be taken as a sort of year's mind, *in memoriam* W.P. Most of the original readers of the book would feel some curiosity about Max, an incipient legend, incredibly young, yet with such an old head on his shoulders, so controlled and so audacious, so wise and so silly, so talented and attractive and well behaved most but not all of the time. What will Max make of Pater, his fellow Oxonian, the stylist of stylists, an elder friend of Oscar's as Max is a younger, who intended to contribute to the *Yellow Book* as Max had in fact? If Max had his way to make, it could be assumed to be along Pater's way, and his tiny *Works* jump in ahead of the confidently expected collected works of Pater. We begin to read. The opening sentences are notably oblique:

> In the year of grace 1890, and in the beautiful autumn of that year, I was a freshman at Oxford. I remember how my tutor asked me what lectures I wished to attend, and how he laughed when I said that I wished to attend the lectures of Mr. Walter Pater.

One forms a momentary picture of an aesthetic youth brought up short by a hearty unappreciative tutor – an anticipation perhaps of Evelyn Waugh and C.R.M.F. Cruttwell or John Betjeman and C.S. Lewis. Read on.

> Also I remember how, one morning soon after, I went into Ryman's to order some foolish engraving for my room, and

there saw, peering into a portfolio, a small, thick, rock-faced
man, whose top-hat and gloves of *bright* dog-skin struck
one of the many discords in that little city of learning and
laughter. The serried bristles of his moustachio made for
him a false-military air. I think I nearly went down when
they told me that this was Pater.

That there was something the matter with Pater's appearance all agree. Pater himself said he would give ten years of
his life to be handsome; he grew the egregious Kiplingesque
moustache with that in mind (how cruel to say "moustachio"
– and what a curious farrago of romance languages). He is recalled as looking thus while still at school:

> Pater, thin, rather hump-backed, pales, with a most singular
> face, and prematurely whiskered. He had an overhanging
> forehead, deep set mild eyes, a nose very low in the bridge
> and neither Grecian nor Roman; a curious misformation
> of the mouth, resembling slightly some species of ape; and
> those strange whiskers.

Oscar Browning remarks that "Pater's appearance was the reverse of aesthetic," and a lady visitor cannot name him without
adding "(who is far from being as beautiful as his own prose)."
Perhaps he seemed all the uglier because of this expectation,
this disappointment. There may well be the unspoken require-
ment that Walter Pater, as a homosexual (if a homosexual),
ought at least to have been good looking. But it is not just the
ugliness. Some quite ugly men are not recalled as ugly. Carlyle
was craggy – and in Ford Madox Brown's "Work" could pass
for D.H. Lawrence's uncle – and Ruskin somewhat resembled
Holman Hunt's Scapegoat; George Moore, who said that Pater was "an uncouth figure like a figure moulded out of lead,"
was himself, in the eyes of W.B. Yeats, "a man carved out of a
turnip"; Anatole France was as deliberate a stylist as Pater, and

one may admire or deplore his style, but his strange horse-like visage is part of his distinction. Pater cut a better figure in London than in Oxford, to be sure, but one cannot help concluding, with Max, that he was doomed to failure whatever dandiacal steps he might have taken. The smallest possible vignette, the tiniest possible walk-on part is, as it were, all that Max can allow an actor long past it and never very accomplished.[61]

All this, however, is appearance; style for Max is reality. Perhaps this unprepossessing character will prove to be a Helper in the quest for the Holy Grail (which for Max and his set, we recall, is the *mot juste*), perhaps this toad will have a precious jewel in his head, perhaps the style and the doctrine will fare better. Max now draws his silver dagger. "Not that even in those more decadent days of my childhood did I admire the man as a stylist." Max is betrayed into bad syntax for a moment, a rare failing in him (you may say "not that I admired" or "nor did I admire" but must not attempt to straddle the two) – betrayed by glee at the very notion of a decadent childhood, betrayed by *Schadenfreude* at the insulting phrase "the man" – a construction at least as old as Dickens ("the man Snawly" in *Nickleby*, ch. 50), to burst out later that very year in universal execration of "the man Wilde." I conjecture that this snide practice originated in an effort to identify a contemptible person without calling him Mister.

Max continues: "Even then I was angry that he should treat English as a dead language...." Indeed Pater in an essay on "English Literature" had written that "a busy age will hardly educate its writers in correctness. Let its writers make time to write English more as a learned language ...." Max substitutes for "learned," "dead," and continues: "... bored by that sedulous ritual ...." "Sedulous," a word learned by every aspiring stylist from Robert Louis Stevenson, who "played the sedulous ape" to certain choice spirits of the past; and "ritual," to fuse Pater's known interest in High Church ritual with whatever is to be found objectionable in his style; "bored," then, "by that sedulous ritual wherewith he laid out every sentence as in a shrowd – hanging, like a widower, long over its marmoreal beauty or ever he could lay it at length in his book, its sepulcher."[62]

Max was not the first or the last to be made uncomfortable by the funereal tone of Pater. Pater himself, writing of Sir Thomas Browne, says, "it is well, perhaps, that life should be something of a 'meditation upon death': but to many, certainly, Browne's would have seemed too like a lifelong following of one's own funeral." He seems not to have noticed the applicability to himself. John Addington Symonds (who will be not nearly so hostile in later references) wrote in a letter of 1873:

> There is a kind of Death clinging to the man, wh[ich] makes his music (but heavens! how sweet it is!) a little faint & sickly. His view of life gives me the creeps, as old women say. I am sure it is a ghastly sham; & that live by it or not as he may do, his utterance of the theory to the world has in it a wormy hollow-voiced seductiveness of a fiend.

And Lytton Strachey, whom Max was to regard as such a kindred spirit, wrote; in a letter of 1901: "As for Pater, though I have not read much of him he appears to me so deathly – no motion, no vigour – a waxen style."[63]

Scattered through Pater's works are passages that might be termed morbid by such critics as Lady Bracknell. The essentially autobiographical "The Child in the House" remarks on how "with this desire of physical beauty mingled itself early the fear of death," to be intensified later in gazing on dead faces

> as sometimes, afterwards, at the *Morgue* in Paris, or in that fair cemetery at Munich where all the dead must go and lie in state before burial, behind glass windows, among the flowers and incense and holy candles – the aged clergy with their sacred ornaments, the young men in their dancing-

shoes and spotless white linen – after which visits, those waxen, resistless faces would always live with him for many days, making the broadest sunshine sickly.

We know that Pater himself visited the Morgue in Paris; we know too that Vernon Lee, who rather liked Pater, found the house he shared with his sisters "rather *triste*." In one of his earliest essays, on Coleridge (1865, 1880), he observes that "Forms of intellectual and spiritual culture sometimes exercise their subtlest and most artful charm when life is already passing, from them," and on two later occasions he is to use the metaphor of "embalming" in a highly favourable context.[64]

This cult of *Thanatos* is intricated with Pater's ritualism, even to the point of liturgical incorrectness. In *Gaston de la Tour*, Candlemas, surely a joyous ceremony, is spoken of as funereal, its colour penitential violet, and later in the same story the low spirits of the young man fail to rise at Easter:

> The sudden gaieties of Easter morning, the congratulations to the Divine Mother, the sharpness of the recoil from one extreme of feeling to the other, for him never cleared away the Lenten pre-occupation with Christ's death and passion: the empty tomb, with the white clothes lying, was still a tomb: there was no human warmth in the "spiritual body": the white flowers, after all, were those of a funeral, with a mortal coldness, amid the loud Alleluias, which refused to melt at the startling summons, any more than the earth will do in the March morning because we call it Spring.

Edmund Gosse even quotes Pater as remarking that the presence of the Reserved Sacrament in churches "gave them all the sentiment of a house where lay a dead friend." No sense in him of "the life of the building." Add to this the high mortality rate of intelligent, sensitive and handsome young men in Pater's writings and one can see why Max writes: "From that laden air, the so cadaverous murmur of that sanctuary, I would hook it at the beck of any jade.[65]

Max has by no means finished with Pater in this essay: he has more to say about – and in imitation of – his style. He uses a little Greek, untranslated, as Pater does, comical in the context but correct, and then makes a most surprising disclosure:

> At school I had read *Marius the Epicurean* in bed and with a dark lantern. Indeed, I regarded it mainly as a tale of adventure, quite as fascinating as *Midshipman Easy*, and far less hard to understand, because there were no nautical terms in it. Marryat, moreover, never made me wish to run away to sea, whilst certainly Pater did make me wish for more "colour" in the curriculum....

We know that Max while at school read *Pendennis* and *Vanity Fair* and *The Newcomes* as well, but we must think of him as reading *Marius*, excited like Pater's lad by the discovery of Apuleius and the *Pervigilium Veneris*, but acquiescing (as Marius did to the old observances of the religion of Numa) to the "slow revolution" of his school's "wheel of work and play.[66]

"I felt that at Oxford, when I should be of age to matriculate, a 'variegated dramatic life' was waiting for me. I was not a little too sanguine, alas!" Oxford proved to be "a bit of Manchester through which Apollo had once passed." He is disheartened, in the style of Pater:

> Bitter were the comparisons I drew between my coming to Oxford and the coming of Marius to Rome. Could it be that there was at length no beautiful environment wherein a man might sound the harmonies of his soul? Had civilization made beauty, besides adventure, so rare? I wondered what counsel Pater, insistent always upon contact with comely things, would offer to one who could nowhere find them.

I had been wondering that very day when I went into Ryman's and saw him there.[67]

The ensuing paragraph of renunciation of Pater's doctrines by no means renounces Pater's style. Even the doctrines are rather stretched than renounced when tested by the contrasting world of London with its "swirls, eddies, torrents, violent cross-currents of human activity. What uproar!" And in the "prodigious life of the Prince of Wales ... was there ever so supernal a type, as he, of mere Pleasure?" Talk about filling every moment, living every moment for the moment's sake! The doctrine that haunts this part of "Diminuendo" is that of the brief "Conclusion" to *The Renaissance*, especially its last paragraph, its last sentence – "For art comes to you preparing frankly to give nothing but the highest quality to your moments as they pass, and simply for those moments' sake" – and most especially its last word, a favourite of Pater and all who follow him. What is art, asks Samuel Butler, that it should have a "sake"? Appearing here for the first time in writing is a person, rather a figure, who is to haunt Max's imagination from the Nineties into old age, the Prince of Wales, afterward King Edward VII, whom Max was to draw sixty times between 1896 and 1953, Clever Max! to see that the philosophy of life of Albert Edward, Prince of Wales can be set beside that of Walter Horatio Pater. It is Pater's demure tune played on the saxophone, that instrument coeval with the Prince.[68]

However, Max is wise enough to recognize that he cannot keep pace with the Prince, being "shod neither with rank nor riches" – well chosen word, "shod": though beyond his means, under his feet. And so he makes a resolution:

It was, for me, merely a problem how I could best avoid "sensations," "pulsations," and "exquisite moments" that were not purely intellectual. I would not attempt to combine both kinds, as Pater seemed to fancy a man might.

Having chosen early retirement, the earliest ever, he ends this essay and the book as he had opened, with an epigraph from Pater, thus: "to be outmoded is to be a classic, if one has written well. I have acceded to the hierarchy of good scribes and rather like my niche." Are we not intended (and do we not all fail) to recall that "Winckelmann himself explains the motives of his life when he says, 'It will be my highest reward, if posterity acknowledges that I have written worthily'."[69]

Pater is present at the beginning of *Works* and at the end; he is also there in most of its seven essays. The opening page of the first, "Dandies and Dandies" speaks of a "sentiment of style," a "surer delicacy," of "mysteries," and (I am sure in conscious parody of Pater, as the others may be accidental) of "unbridled decorum" and "decorous debauchery" – echoing such phrases of Pater as "a refined and comely decadence," or "a certain refined voluptuousness," or "passionate coldness." For good measure, Max throws in a German word, untranslated (and uncapitalized), *einsamkeit*, just as Pater not seldom did. The essay on George IV exclaims, "How strange it must be to be a king? How delicate and difficult a task it is to judge him!" (There speaks the future King Auberon.) Max generally eschews the words one thinks of as Pater's own – the adjectives, quaint, refined, dainty, subtle, winsome, curious, hidden, weary, secret, cunning; the nouns, sensation, sentiment, charm, fascination, mystery, spell, experience, magic; the verbs, to interpenetrate, to interfuse; but here are two very special ones in emphatic proximity – strange, delicate.[70]

Pater, as we have observed, is inexorably present in "Diminuendo"; startling is his absence from "1880" – as if exorcised. The essay is really about the decade, not just the year, and Oscar Wilde, yes, is there, and aestheticism, yes, but Pater, who had published *The Renaissance* in the late Seventies and had *Marius* and *Imaginary Portraits* in the making, no. Max was doubtless saving him for the special treatment in "Diminuendo."

Turning to the next collection, *More* (1899), we find a continuing but much diminished presence of Pater, mainly in a single word that crops up, or barks out, in no fewer than six of the essays. In Pater and in Max, and it seems in them almost alone, we find always the explosive "Well!", never the reflective and dawdling "Well!" It is as much a Pater signature as ending an epigram with "That is all" is a Wilde signature, and Max forges both.

Pater is mentioned four times. At Madame Tussaud's, Max writes, "my visit may have been a 'sensation' or an 'experience,' or both, but it was not at all nice." A Pateresque context being established, he considers the wax figures as statues:

> But statuary, as Pater pointed out, in a pregnant (if rather uncouth) sentence, moves us to emotion, "not by accumulation of detail, but by abstracting from it." I think that waxworks fail because they are not made within any of those "exquisite limitations" of colour, texture, proportions, to which all visual arts must be subjected.

Again, in the essay on Ouida, he observes that "Too much art is, of course, as great an obstacle as too little art; and Pater, in his excessive care for words, is as obscure to most people as are Carlyle and Browning, in their carelessness. "He begins the next paragraph with "Well!" The essay on the literary cult of the child anticipates a publisher's blurb – "Mr. Pater's most exquisite achievement is *The Child in the House*." And the last essay, "The Case of Prometheus," recalls that "some one suspiciously like Apollo has been seen herding sheep in Picardy," an allusion to Pater's *Apollo in Picardy*.[71]

After this, Pater's appearances in Max's pages are, we may say, desultory. In his dramatic criticism he indulges in a "Well! (as Pater himself would have said)" and on another occasion refers to him admiringly and at some length as an "exquisite prose amateur," the same point being made in the essay on

"Whistler's Writing" (1904): "all of the much that we admire in Walter Pater's prose comes of the lucky chance that he was an amateur and never knew his business." Much? Yes, when in the essay on "The Naming of Streets" (1902) Max imagines Walter Pater and Walter Besant changing surnames at birth: then "'Walter Besant' would have signified a prose style sensuous in its severity, an exquisitely patient scholarship, an exquisitely sympathetic way of criticism." Not at all an unadmiring tribute. However, Max does allow himself two last, delicious liberties. Pater was something of a sobersides. If Lionel Johnson, who, like Max, read Pater in boyhood, could celebrate "quiet mirth" and "veritable fun" in his master, the only mirth in either is so quiet as hardly to be mirth at all, the only fun so veritable as hardly to be fun. Max and his friends in contrast enjoyed the rowdy entertainment of the music hall, and on one occasion he has the impudence to speak of its limelight as a "hard gemlike flame." The other final *jeu d'esprit*: writing about a third legendary figure, Sarah Bernhardt, he recalls two others: "In Queen Victoria I saw always something of that uncanny symbolism which Mr. Pater saw in the portrait of Mona Lisa, Hers, too, surely, was the head upon which all the ends of the world were come, and the eyelids were a little weary...."[72]

Pater may at the beginning have taught Max to write carefully; if Max continued to write carefully all his life, Pater did not long continue to teach him how. Let us not end on such a diminuendo but return briefly to "Diminuendo" and its quite extraordinary animus at the year's mind of Pater's death. In March, 1894, Max wrote to Reggie Turner from Oxford a newsy latter about Bosie Douglas and John Lane ("in very new dogskin gloves") and Will Rothenstein, who

is up and has done a lithograph of me for the Oxford Series; it will appear in the next number with Walter Pater – the two stylists. It is rather touching: you know how angry old Henry Acland was at the libellous portrait of him and how that

Walter Pater refused to sit at all? Well, poor Rothenstein has turned idealist, in consequence – has done a second thing of old Henry who, no longer an old village-dotard, appears exactly like Gladstone, only far firmer, and Walter Pater, who as you know is a kind of hump-back *manqué*, figures as a young guardsman with curly mustachios – just what Kendal must have looked like twenty years ago. Isn't it rather touching? I too who write am a child of fifteen and quite god-like.

Pater died, unexpectedly, later that year, and Max in notes on Oscar Wilde's conversation, records this: "Day of announcement of Pater's death – Laughed – cut off in flower of middle age." Of the "two stylists," the younger is clearly a resentful rival of the elder; the jottings are so curt that it is impossible to be sure whether the heartlessness is Oscar's only or shared by Max. The guilt of the giggle (I consider it sinful) is predominantly Wilde's: he owed a great deal to Pater and had far outstripped him in the world of publicity whereas Max still had his way to make and one "lion of milder roar" no longer stood in that way. Still, at the moment he began the long pregnancy of "Diminuendo," Max strikes one as a bit pert. His grave hardly slept in, Pater should not have been so used by a fellow Oxonian. As the young surrealists danced at the grave of Anatole France, so young Max took his congee of Pater with levity.[73]

This is the place for an elaborate Freudian cadenza, especially given Pater's surname, but the reader can supply it as easily as I can, and so I take it as sounded. Besides, Max lost his real father about the time Pater died, to his real grief, and Pater was never a father, rather an uncle figure he expected to find helpful but found blocking.

Once Max retired to Rapallo, Pater lingered only as a ghost might without menace. Rossetti's "Circle" might easily have been drawn with wide enough circumference to include him, but it wasn't, though Wilde and Whistler are there. His footstep is unheard in Zuleika Dobson's Oxford, but memory fetches him to view, "Oxford, 1911, taking his walk through the Meadows," "moustachios," "*bright* dog-skin gloves," and all. Some time, any time, Max amused himself by inventing quotations from reviews and entering them in his copy of Pater's *Renaissance*:

Some opinions of the Press

"Something of raucousness but much of vitality.... Mr. Pater
does not mince his words." – *Spectator*.

"Thor's hammer on Vulcan's anvil." – *Manchester Guardian*.

"At once a scourge and a purge." – *Wigan Remembrances*.[74]

The Mirror of the Past, as reconstructed by Lawrence Danson from the collection of Robert H. Taylor in the Princeton University Library, does not mention Pater, but Max himself in a radio broadcast of 1955, "Hethway Speaking," which draws on anecdotes intended for that abandoned venture, maintains until the end that he is recalling conversations with Sylvester Hethway in 1895. Here the very "period" recollections of Swinburne, Meredith, Rossetti, Whistler, Carlyle, and Morris, lead up to the last one, of Pater, and it is by no means an anticlimax. In contrast to the harsh and dismissive year's mind in "Diminuendo," the touch here, in the fifty-years' mind, is affable, almost affectionate. "He liked to be amiably rallied, to be teased a little by his friends," Hethway observes:

> He earnestly counselled the young to be – what was the famous phrase? – "be present always at the focus where the greatest number of vital forces unite in their greatest energy." And he himself could not stand Kensington High Street. He very solemnly warned the young that "to form habits is failure in life." I suggested to him one day that in the next edition of his book he ought to add a foot-note: "In life, however, there are worse things than failure: for example, not having one's cup of tea, with a slice of thin bread

and butter, at five o'clock *punctually*." He laughed gently and said, "That is a shrewd jest at *me*, Hethway; but not at the sincerity of my doctrine." And of course he was quite right there. No man was more sincere in his efforts to make people as unlike himself as possible.

There we may let Pater rest.[75]

Before we move to the second half of this long excursus, toward a discussion of G.K. Chesterton and Oscar Wilde on the pattern of Max and Pater, it may be observed that Wilde played a considerable part in Max's life and art but never as a rival and only for a short time as a compeer. It is particularly instructive to compare the Wilde of "A Peep into the Past" (written 1893–4) with the Pater of "Diminuendo" (written 1895). Max had privately commented on the growing coarseness, extravagance, and befuddlement of Wilde in the period just before his fall, and his famous caricature of him says the same thing. In his essay on "The Spirit of Caricature" (1901) he stoutly stated that "Caricature implies no moral judgment on its subject," meaning by this that it avoids tedious moralizing. More than that he cannot mean: if half of his caricatures contain no appreciable moral judgment, the other half are equally divided between indulgent rebuke and stern rebuke. In the prose skit, which has the force of caricature, apart from the few pointed references to a succession of messenger boys and "the quickly receding *frou-frou* of tweed trousers," the satiric technique is the time-honoured one of "praise undeserved is scandal in disguise": he presents Oscar as rising before dawn to work on his jokes and is careful to stress all the middle-class virtues of the elderly gentleman he is pretending to interview. The scandal made it unpublishable, but if it had appeared as Max originally intended, perhaps in *The Yellow Book*, it could hardly have failed to delight its readers, Oscar chief among them, whereas if Pater could have read "Diminuendo," he would only have been pained.[76]

Wilde's writings are a clear influence on some of Max's. The very early "Pervasion of Rouge" is a small embroidery on Oscar's central idea of the superiority of art to nature. "The Happy Hypocrite" can stand unabashed beside Wilde's fairy stories. A.V. Laider's chiromancy recalls *Lord Arthur Savile's Crime*, and Zuleika (sporting the name of Potiphar's wife and of Goethe's inamorata, though alas the American girl pronounces it Zuleeka) – Zuleika Dobson is the closest Max can come to Salome.

Wilde's wit and Max's also have clear affinities. Max's is (to borrow a word from Pater) daintier, Oscar's (let's be outrageous) more earnest. Max took his own course as stylist, soon moving away from the characteristically Wildean inverted truism, and as he did so, Oscar is supplanted as hero by Rossetti. The last plate in *Rossetti and his Circle* shows Oscar Wilde bringing word of Rossetti to the Americans, but the artist and the reader see this as the close of one great lifetime rather than as the beginning of another.[77]

In the time of Max's youth, however, Oscar is seen as the embodiment of a life devoted to art – much more than the disappointing Pater, more even than Herbert Beerbohm Tree, who as an impresario was half artist, half businessman. Tree, who produced some of Oscar's plays, had introduced his half-brother Max (twenty years his junior) to the playwright, and Oscar became, not a seducer or a bogey, but a big exuberant helper, another half-brother of avuncular age. (Max had other elder half-brothers, one of them named – what, else? – Ernest.) Max's closest lifelong friends, Reggie Turner and Will Rothenstein, were small men, Will being so notably short that he refers to Max as "tall." Max himself was five foot eight and three quarters, which is "medium" in any tailor's book. But Oscar Wilde and Herbert Beerbohm Tree and G.K. Chesterton were all giants, gentle giants, giants of tremendous presence. Let Herbert speak for all three: when asked how he was, he would reply "I'm radiant!"[78]

As Max slipped his silver dagger into Pater, so Chesterton must draw his sword-stick on Wilde; as Max's engagement with Wilde's personality and ideas has been briefly dealt with, so can G.K.C.'s with Pater's. In his book on Dickens (1906), Chesterton, preparing for the entrance of his hero, draws a vivid contrast between the temper of the early nineteenth century and the late:

> The first period was full of evil things, but it was full of hope. The second period, the *fin de siècle*, was even full (in some sense) of good things. But it was occupied in asking what was the good of good things. Joy itself became joyless; and the fighting of Cobbett was happier than the feasting of Walter Pater.

No hint here of Max's personal disenchantment. Pater is not a person but a style and a doctrine, neither of which has been seriously entertained. In *Heretics* (1905) he says of moments of happiness, "once look at them as moments after Pater's manner, and they become as cold as Pater and his style." He continues:

> Pater's mistake is revealed in his most famous phrase. He asks us to burn with a hard, gem-like flame. Flames are never hard and never gem-like – they cannot be handled or arranged. So human emotions are never hard and never gem-like; they are always dangerous, like flame, to touch or even to examine.

Chesterton may have missed Pater's point here (or one possible reading of Pater) if the flame is the light struck off from the gem, from the "crystal man" – and he may have seen it in those odd little verses that refer to Max's "odd crystalline sense."[79]

To say that Pater is "Ruskin without the prejudices, that is, without the funny parts" is right on the mark and itself very funny; the whole passage from *The Victorian Age in Literature* is as acute a criticism of consumers' aestheticism as can be found in short compass, and the immediately following discussion of the Mona Lisa passage articulates well the resistance of any genuine Christian feeling or any sound Christian doctrine to subsumption into aesthetic syncretism. But Chesterton's treatment of Pater is never vehement, and when in his book on Stevenson he remarks that "it really did seem preposterous to many that a serious literary artist of the age of Pater should devote himself to rewriting Penny Dreadfuls," there is no evident doubt in his mind that Pater was a serious artist of sufficient stature to give his name to an age. This is reinforced by his late reference to Pater, in 1931:

> A man speaking of fine English prose in my boyhood would probably have mentioned both Pater and Newman. I have lately heard an amazing number of people sneering at Pater; I have not heard many people, or indeed any people, sneering at Newman.

Never a pagan in his admiration of Pater, he is not now joining the pack of pagans who sneer at him.[80]

There is a passage in *Heretics* that will serve as a bridge from Pater, who never mattered much to Chesterton, to Wilde, who was always a serious concern:

> Walter Pater said that we were all under sentence of death, and the only course was to enjoy exquisite moments simply for those moments' sake. The same lesson was taught by the very powerful and very desolate philosophy of Oscar Wilde.

Carpe diem is the religion of unhappy people, a desolate philosophy but, Chesterton admits, a powerful one.[81]

Of the writers who have left record of growing up in the Nineties, Chesterton is one of the few to have felt sharply the

moral and spiritual danger of the age. His friend and schoolmate E.C. Bentley does not bear or sing the burden of the
Decadence, and a close friend of later years, Maurice Baring, in
one of his *Lost Lectures*, gives a pleasant account of the decade,
stressing hard work and innocent frolics and ordinariness.
Any decade can – and perhaps should – be made to disappear
into the flux of time: a decade is, after all, only a revolution of
the sun multiplied quite arbitrarily by the ten fingers of the
hand. Two drops of sceptical aqua regia. Rudyard Kipling, who
sprang into world-wide prominence in the Nineties but, with
his appeal to hearties and to empire builders, seemed to embody everything counter to the aesthetes and decadents, was
Burne-Jones's nephew; more surprising than that, he is at pains
to describe his heroic young scamp, Stalky, and his company as
unmistakably aesthetic though not decadent. Again, the florist
who devised the green carnation and supplied it as a sort of
badge to Oscar Wilde and his minions was the brother of the
sensible and liberal-minded socialist and feminist, Mrs. Hubert Bland, better known as E. Nesbit, creator of the engaging
Bastable children who in the Nineties are fully occupied with
seeking treasure and trying to be good, with never a thought of
green carnations.[82]

The special narrow sense of the Nineties and the Ninetyish,
under those names, became current shortly before the Great
War. As one of its survivors, W. B. Yeats, observed, most of
the "Tragic Generation" had died before their time – Wilde,
Beardsley, Ernest Dowson, Lionel Johnson, Hubert Crack-
enthorpe, John Davidson. Arthur Symons faded from the picture; John Gray trod the opposite path to Dorian and entered
the priesthood, and Yeats himself moved on to new concerns
and a new style. Others were long to survive the decade: if they
had not, perhaps we would be accommodating within our conception of the Nineties "The Turn of the Screw" (1898), "Heart
of Darkness" (1899), or the more horrifying of H.G. Wells's
early scientific romances.[83]

Really to belong to the Nineties (hindsight tells us) one must be a Londoner by birth or choice, a nocturnal animal given to solitude or harlots, to raffish café life or the Café Royal. The works (or names) of Balzac, Baudelaire, Théophile Gautier certainly, of Verlaine and Huysmans perhaps, would count for more in our conversation than their contemporaries among English writers, though James and Meredith, Stevenson and George Moore are read and admired. French Impressionism is known and talked about, and Whistler is still news. Wraithlike Beardsley and fleshly Wilde make their astounding appearances and disappearances. Both are taken up and promoted by John Lane of The Bodley Head and by Leonard Smithers, publishers of what may be called the shallow Nineties and the deep Decadence.[84]

Max was a mature twenty-three and a published writer and caricaturist in 1895 at the time of Oscar Wilde's fall. A child who put his hand in the hole of the asp and was not stung, he had been a familiar of the Wilde circle, agreeable though somewhat aloof, well armed as satirist and caricaturist. Decadence, from the time of *Dorian* (1890), had been grossly melodramatized, with much connivance by the decadents themselves, and grossly oversold. Max was not a plunger in this market and was only slightly nipped in the crash: as a "mulierast" (a word he adopted from Robert Ross – the opposite of a pederast) he was not himself threatened. His reaction to the arrest of Wilde is quiet: he writes from Chicago to Reggie Turner asking to be kept informed, he expresses continuing friendship and sympathy, he sends his *Works* and *The Happy Hypocrite* to Wilde, and he refrains from publishing "A Peep into the Past" or from republishing the caricature in which Oscar seemed indeed to be "posing as a somdomite." "Enoch Soames" (1916) is his considered evocation and judgment of the Nineties: it is all there – the Café Royal and the café in Soho, a book of verse called *Fungoids* and a book of verse untitled, Catholic diabolism, the absurdity and pathos of the decadent look and pose, and even (as the centennial of Enoch's disappointment in the Reading Room of the British Museum inexorably approached) a fellow-feeling.[85]

Chesterton was an immature twenty-one at the time of the Wilde scandal, having just left the Slade School to work in a publishing house. Their two years difference in age made all the difference. Max took part in the Nineties as their youngest participant. G.K.C. began his experience of life by shrinking (shrinking!) from decadence before expanding toward orthodoxy. (By an accident of classification the Library of Congress places G.K.C. among the Victorians, near Carlyle, and Max among the Moderns, near Brendan Behan.) Having no experience of the Oxford, literary, theatrical, and social circles in which Max moved and which brought him into casual friendship with a celebrity who was good company and generous of his talents and substance, Chesterton must have felt bludgeoned by the vileness uncovered by the court proceedings no less than by the Philistine hypocrisy of the press and the cruelty of the sentence. There is an early clerihew by Bentley in a manuscript collection not later than 1893, illustrated by his schoolmate G.K.C.

> Mr. Oscar Wilde
> Got extremely riled.
> He ejaculated, "Blow me
> If I don't write 'Salomé'."

A couple of Bentley's words have taken a tumble in the century since he wrote them, but it is a jolly production: the drawing shows, not Wilde, but a headless corpse and Salome holding the head that has just been whisked off, but not doing anything worse with it.[86]

This young illustrator, outwardly full of fun, living in the give-and-take of comradeship, learning from Walt Whitman to embrace his fellow man, must have seen in Wilde's "feasting with panthers" something malignant, counter to ordinary goodness wherever it exists, and allied to an inner threat to himself personally. In his last book, the *Autobiography* (1936), he recalls this dark threat, being careful not to blame "the atmosphere of the Decadents, and their perpetual hints of the luxurious horrors of paganism" for what in himself ran parallel to them:

> But anyhow, it is true that there was a time when I reached that condition of moral anarchy within, in which a man says, in the words of Wilde, that "Atys with the blood-stained knife were better than the thing I am." I have never indeed felt the faintest temptation to the particular madness of Wilde; but I could at this time imagine the worst and wildest disproportions and distortions of more normal passion; the point is that the whole mood was overpowered and oppressed with a sort of congestion of imagination.

Closer to the time is the dedicatory poem to *Thursday* (1908), where G.K.C. reminds E.C. Bentley of their boyhood days "when the world was old and ended" and "art admired decay": there was "a sick cloud upon the soul," but they resisted and defied it, along with their giant helpers, Whitman and Stevenson.[87]

Chesterton's first published writings are two books of verse, one nonsensical, the other serious, neither touched by the language or tone of decadence. Almost at the same time he found his vein as an essayist in *The Defendant*, written as articles and collected in a book in 1901. Oscar Wilde is named very soon – and as we shall see is a presence throughout:

> One great decadent, who is now dead, published a poem some time ago in which he powerfully summed up the whole spirit of the movement, by declaring that he could stand in the prison yard and entirely comprehend the feelings of a man about to be hanged:

"For he that lives more lives than one
More deaths than one must die."

And the end of all this is that maddening horror of unreality which descends upon all decadents, and compared with which physical pain would have the freshness of a youthful thing. The one hell which imagination must conceive as most hellish is to be eternally acting a play without even the narrowest and dirtiest greenroom in which to be human. And this is the condition of the decadent, of the aesthete, of the free-lover. To be everlastingly passing through dangers which we know cannot scathe us, to be taking oaths which we know cannot bind us, to be defying enemies who we know cannot conquer us – this is the grinning tyranny of decadence which is called freedom.

This is not to make a scapegoat of Wilde but to attack a doctrine, as is clear from *Heretics* (1905): Oscar Wilde "we fêted and flattered because he preached such an attitude, and then broke his heart, in penal servitude because he carried it out."[88]

A striking passage in the book on Shaw (1909) proves that G.K.C., like W.B. Yeats, saw Wilde as no mere voluptuary but as essentially a man of action and conflict, his life as exemplary as Shaw who "always challenges like a true Green Islander."

An even stronger instance of this national trait can be found in another Irishman, Oscar Wilde. His philosophy (which was vile) was a philosophy of ease, of acceptance, and luxurious illusion; yet, being Irish, he could not help putting it in pugnacious and propagandist epigrams. He preached his softness with hard decision; he praised pleasure in the words most calculated to give pain. This armed insolence, which was the noblest thing about him, was also the Irish thing; he challenged all comers.

It was also, of course, the Shavian and the Chestertonian thing, the thing that separated him from the other Decadents, from Pater, and from Max.[89]

His fullest treatment of Wilde as man and writer occurs near the end of *The Victorian Age in Literature* (1913). Speaking of the Aesthetes of the '80s and the Decadents of the '90s, he observes neatly that "the same bandmaster, Oscar Wilde, walked in front of the first procession wearing a sunflower, and in front of the second procession wearing a green carnation," and he conjures up "the image of Wilde lolling like an elegant leviathan on a sofa." Wilde's poems (with one exception) he finds to be on the boundary of the absurd and the pathetic, and Wilde's taste a mixture of sensibility and coarseness, though "there was a sort of power – or at least weight – in his coarseness. His lapses were those proper to the one good thing he really was, an Irish swashbuckler – a fighter. Some of the Roman Emperors might have had the same luxuriousness and yet the same courage." By the time G.K.C. placed the words "weight" and "coarseness" in such close juxtaposition, he had himself grown to enormous girth: he and Wilde were about the same height, six foot two or three, and probably the two largest writers in English literature. Either of them, without genius, could have been merely gross. Their nimbleness of mind and cultivation of paradox are compensation. Again, both must have chosen early in life not to be ogres and maintained the habit of being gentle and considerate giants. Whistler and Max never had so to choose to be kind and one chose definitely not to be. This really must be the last mention of size, hard though it is to resist in the context.[90]

A dozen years will pass before he returns to any significant consideration of Wilde. This will be in the book on Stevenson (1927); the subject, their common master in narrative, will draw them together. G.K.C. observes early in the book, with justice though without notable originality, that Wilde will be remembered as a man and not as an artist, and at the end, with a kind of justice that is not much help to anyone, that Stevenson made better use of his bad health than Wilde of his good. Between them is a strong passage on Stevenson's historically crucial reaction and counter-attack against European pessimism, that cultic and crepuscular mood masquerading as a doctrine:

> Anyhow, in that period we might almost say that pessimism was another name for culture. Cheerfulness was associated with the Philistine, like the broad grin with the bumpkin. Pessimism could be read between the lines of the lightest triolet or the most elegant essay. Any one who really remembers that time will admit that the world was much more hopeful after the worst of its wars than it was not long before Mr. H.G. Wells, whose genius had just been discovered by Henley, was very much older than he is now. He was prophesying that the outline of history would end, not in communism, but in cannibalism. He was prophesying the end of the world: a crack of doom not even cheerful enough to be a day of judgement. Oscar Wilde, who perhaps filled up more room, both in mind and body, than anyone else on that stage at that moment, expressed his philosophy in that bitter parable in which Christ seeks to comfort a man weeping and is answered, "Lord, I was dead and you raised me to life; what else can I do but weep?"[91]

Here Chesterton is displaying an interest in Wilde the writer as well as Wilde the moralist and example. They have a surprising amount in common as literary men. To take an unemphatic instance first. Both were fascinated by anarchism, as Stevenson was, and Conrad – a phenomenon that Pater and Max took not the slightest interest in. While the G.K.C, of *Thursday* probably had not read Wilde's early play *Vera, or the Anarchists*, which was not readily available until 1909, both works catch the starry-eyed youthful desperation and futility of the anarchists, and, what is more important, the plot of both turns on the necessary penetration of the anarchist world by the existing order.[92]

More clearly Chesterton takes up the challenge hurled by Wilde in the essays of *Intentions*. By the way, the interlocutors in "The Decay of Lying" are Cyril and Vivian, the names of Oscar's two sons, but in "The Critic as Artist" they are Ernest (that figures) and (O my prophetic soul!) Gilbert. G.K.C. comes manfully to the defence of nature, not of the obvious beauty of what Oscar would call "a foolish sunset," but of the ugliness, the babyishness, of nature, in what is surely one of the most unusual arguments ever to be effectively adduced:

> But the fact that nature is beautiful in the sense that a dado or a Liberty curtain is beautiful is only one of her charms, and almost an accidental one .... Has the poet, for whom nature means only rose and lilies, ever heard a pig grunting? It is a noise that does a man good – a strong, snorting, imprisoned noise, breaking its way out of unfathomable dungeons through every possible outlet and organ. It might be the voice of the earth itself, snoring in its mighty sleep. This is the deepest, the oldest, the most wholesome and religious sense of the value of nature – the value which comes from her immense babyishness. She is as top-heavy, as grotesque, as solemn, and as happy as a child. The mood does come when we see all her shapes like shapes that a baby scrawls upon a slate – simple, rudimentary, a million years older and stronger than the whole disease that is called art.

One regrets that Oscar did not live to say "I wish I had said that."[93]

About *The Picture of Dorian Gray*, the book that launched the Nineties, Wilde admitted, with only partial irony, that it was marred by excessive moralising. It is a chronicle of guilt and debility, it is obsessed with time and change and death, it is an aesthete's *Eric, or Little by Little.* If Chesterton had only laboured over the details of *Manalive* (1912) as Wilde had laboured over *Dorian*, how much more clearly one could see how the lugubrious downward direction of the one is matched by the levity, almost levitation, of the other, how innocence answers guilt and debility is matched by bounce. Both are Stevensonian romances, marked by opulence of style, lavish colour-coding, melodramatic highlighting; both are serious and improving books, Dorian continuing the sombre tone of *Dr. Jekyll*, *Manalive* in the romping vein of some of the *New Arabian Nights*.[94]

Taking a first-class degree, Oscar might have remained at Oxford, and such a piece as "The Rise of Historical Criticism," if coined into an academic career, might have earned him a worthy place among forgotten Oxford dons. A century later, how difficult it would have been for him to avoid the up escalator of Academe: he would have gone on to the doctorate and postdoctoral fellowships and star performances in the academic big time – no stopping him; Chesterton too, come to think of it, once English studies got under way. Instead, he made his living, as G.K.C. was to follow him in doing, by journalism: his reviews and miscellaneous writings fill three volumes, G.K.C.'s ten times that number. In both cases this means of livelihood entailed a readiness to write and a desire to please, and the latter required a sense of audience and the habit of projecting a personality in the public eye. Max managed in similar circumstances to remain always "cosy," but Oscar and G.K.C. were impelled on occasion to speak out – Chesterton in his attacks on eugenics and other evils, his enquiry into what's wrong with the world, his labours in the cause of Distributism, Wilde in *The Soul of Man under Socialism*, widely distributed, and greatly cherished by the downtrodden in Europe, by his well-considered letters on prison reform, and by his *Ballad of Reading Gaol*, which Chesterton praised as "the only real thing" he ever wrote and more democratic than the socialists.[95]

Chesterton to my knowledge does not take notice of *De Profundis* (1905), with its recriminations and parade of repentance, in which the "lord of language" professes to have "no words in which to express my anguish and my shame[,]" ably using the rhetorical (especially romantic) trope of not being able to write the work one is writing. As for true humility, Oscar knew no more of it than – you or I do; and perhaps G.K.C. was humble enough not to take advantage of the wretched man on that score.[96]

An article on "Good Stories Spoilt by Great Writers" (undated) argues that "the mere fact that some fable has passed through a master mind" is no guarantee of its having reached definitive form – witness Shakespeare's treatment of the Lear story, Goethe's of Faust, Wagner's of Tannhauser, and "lastly, (to take a much smaller case)" Wilde's of Salome:

What strikes me most about Wilde's *Salome* is that it is startlingly inartistic. It spoils the whole point of a particularly artistic incident. The brilliant bitterness of the old Bible story consists in the complete innocence and indifference of the dancing girl. A subtle despot was plotting a statesmanlike clemency; a secretive Queen was plotting savage vengeance. A dancer (a mere child, I always fancied) was the daughter of the vengeful Queen and danced before the diplomatic despot. In riotous relaxation he asked the little girl to name any present she liked. Bewildered with such fairy-tale benevolence, the girl ran to ask her mother what she should choose; the patient and pitiless Queen saw her chance and asked for the death of her enemy. In place of this strong, ironic tale of a butterfly used as a hornet, *Salome* has some sickly and vulgar business of the dancer being in love with the Prophet. I am not sure, about its being bad morality; for its morality is its effect on mankind. But I know it is bad art; for its art is its effect on me.

May I adjudicate? It makes a better story the Bible's way and Chesterton's. It makes a better opera Wilde's way and Strauss's.[97]

In many respects Chesterton and Wilde are comparable and equal. They match fiction for fiction, essay for essay, argument for argument, personality for personality. But not play for play, and that is perhaps why Bernard Shaw tried so urgently to persuade his friend and sparring partner to write plays, with only limited success. The goofy nobleman in *Magic* is in the best Wildean vein, and the plot of *The Judgement of Dr. Johnson* is contrived in a way that Wilde would recognize. That is all.[98]

That is all. Favourite trick of style of Oscar Wilde for ending an epigram or, better, a string of epigrams. What remains to be done is to consider the two as epigrammatists, as the two supreme masters of the paradox in English. Their affinity in this regard, by the way, is recognized by Jorge Luis Borges, who has adjacent essays on the two in *Other Inquisitions* and mentions Chesterton in the one on Wilde.[99]

Let Chesterton begin with a reminiscence of the world of what might be called the Lumpenintelligentsia:

> I remember a venerable man with a very long beard who seemed to live at one of these clubs. At intervals he would hold up his hand as if for silence and preface his remarks by saying, "A Thought." And then he would say something that sounded as if a cow had suddenly spoken in the drawing-room. I remember once a silent and much-enduring man ... who could bear it no longer and cried with a sort of expiring gasp, "But, Good God, man, you don't call that a *thought*, do you?"

He continues, closing in on Oscar Wilde:

> It does sometimes happen that a man of real talent has a weakness for flattery, even the flattery of fools. He would

rather say something that silly people think clever than something which only clever people could perceive to be true. Oscar Wilde was a man of this type. When he said somewhere that an immoral woman is the sort of woman a man never gets tired of, he used a phrase so baseless as to be perfectly pointless. Everybody knows that a man may get tired of a whole procession of immoral women, especially if he is an immoral man. That was "a Thought"; otherwise something to be uttered, with uplifted hand, to people who could not think at all. In their poor muddled minds there was some vague connection between wit and cynicism; so they never applauded him so warmly as a wit, as when he was cynical without being witty. But when he said, "A cynic is a man who knows the price of everything and the value of nothing," he made a statement (in excellent epigrammatic form) which really meant something. But it would have meant his own immediate dethronement if it could have been understood by those who only enthroned him for being cynical.

Without denying that Chesterton himself sometimes comes up with "A Thought," most often he is precise in the Wildean way of which he writes, "Wilde knew how to say the precise thing which, whether true or false, is irresistible. As for example, 'I can resist everything but temptation.'" Yes, as for example, "Anything worth doing at all is worth doing badly."[100]

It should on the face of it be possible simply to juxtapose comparable epigrams and paradoxes by the two to see their kinship and rivalry. They might have been cited without regard for date or occasion. After all, none of Oscar's was designed with any thought of G.K.C. or the likes of G.K.C. (there were no likes before him); and any of G.K.C.'s might have been in answer to Oscar. In 1986 a substantial collection of *The Quotable Chesterton* appeared, well selected and well introduced, and in 1989 *The Fireworks of Oscar Wilde*, equally well selected and well introduced – by the Chestertonian, Owen Dudley Edwards. I find, however, on making the attempt, that it will not do. This is in spite of the fact that Chesterton's deeply engrained habit of style, which becomes a cast of mind, is clearly and from the beginning influenced predominantly by Wilde: the turned sentence, the surprising twist of argument, the concern never to bore the reader, always to exploit the full entertainment value of ideas and notions and phrases – all these link the two. But there is a great contrast too, that makes quotation of Wilde easy and effective, of Chesterton, in the same context, hard to begin and hard to leave off.[101]

To put the contrast in terms favourable (perhaps too favourable) to G.K.C. He was ranged against the masters of the destructive or nihilistic paradox, Wilde and Nietzsche notably, and devised for himself as counter-weapon the reconstructive paradox. The inverted truism serves admirably as an instrument for the transvaluation of all values. Used offensively and with careful aim, it has the effect of finality: "that is all." But used by Chesterton in defence of common sense or the perennial philosophy or the Catholic centre, it has the effect of "wait a minute" – let's turn this upside down thing right side up. One tactic works toward the rapid clincher, the other tries to run rings round the enemy. Wilde takes a way of denial, his statements are sharp and glittering, his company is entertaining, even seductive, but he is himself withdrawn. Chesterton is affirmative, expansive, embracing. To be with Wilde is to assist at a firework display, as Mr. Edwards well proves; to be with G.K.C. is to see magic done by daylight. With Wilde, the black sky returns with dazzling blackness and that is all; G.K.C. wants his reader to be more awake and ready to go about his business. Oscar and G.K.C. are like two massive wrestlers, smooth and plump, full of tricks and showmanship, combining good sportsmanship with earnest competition. Today Oscar Wilde is a prophet and martyr of a triumphalist religion, and G.K.C.'s voice is heard among the ruins of a defeated triumphalism. I cannot believe either the victory or the defeat to be as total as they now appear.

And so we return to the ratio: Max is to Pater as G.K.C. is to Wilde – the two observers and appreciators ranged against the two men of opinion and action. To open two large floppy umbrellas, Pater represents aestheticism and style and the 80s, Oscar decadence and paradox and the 90s. A wit like Max found the solemnity of Pater hard to take. A breezy man like G.K.C. must have found oppressive the incense and musk that went with Wilde. For Max, united as it would seem to Pater by Oxford and art and style, the elder, fading man is a blocking character, dull and a little ridiculous. For G.K.C., akin to Wilde in shape of body and mind, in range of interest and paradoxical alertness, the elder man, first preening and flaunting, then suddenly extinguished, is a comrade gone wrong, menacing and pitiable. Max is capable of mischief and G.K.C. of deep anger, but there is a quality of morose delectation that is present in Pater and Wilde that is absent from their successors. And so we return to our chosen pair.

CHAPTER FIVE

Turns on the Tandem

No subject of a caricature by Max could long remain unaware of it. Friends would flock to say, at the same time, that no likeness existed and that the caricaturist was merciless. We know from casual references that G.K.C. looked at examples of Max's art. Chaucer, he says, "like Matthew Arnold in Max's caricature, was not at all times wholly serious" (slightly misquoting the caption, from memory). Again, in an essay on "The False Photographer" (1911), he contrasts the blandness of a photograph of a certain unnamed poet (surely John Davidson) with the strangeness of his appearance in the flesh, and continues:

> I happen to possess a book of Mr. Max Beerbohm's caricatures, one of which depicts the unfortunate poet in question. To say it represents an utterly incredible hobgoblin is to express in faint and inadequate language the licence of its sprawling lines. The authorities thought it strictly safe and scientific to circulate the poet's photograph. They would have clapped me in an asylum if I had asked them to circulate Max's caricature. But the caricature would have been far more likely to find the man.

Lest from this we should surmise that G.K.G. considered Max's drawings so free as to lack form, we may recall an observation in the Chestertonian mode of *reductio ad absurdum*:

Jefferies found in the farcical outlines of fish or bird the notion that they must have been produced without design. To
me this sounds like saying that the caricatures of Max Beerbohm must have been produced without design.

Chesterton accepts by implication the extreme stylization
and distortion in Max's caricatures, say, of Richard Le Gallienne or Arthur Wing Pinero when, in the Father Brown story
"The Man in the Passage," he writes: "His face was somewhat
square, his jaw was square, his shoulders were square, even his
jacket was square. Indeed, in the wild school of caricature then
current, Mr. Max Beerbohm had represented him as a proposi-
tion in the fourth book of Euclid." On this subject, more later,
when we look at Max's caricatures of G.K.C.[102]

As we have seen, Max went along cheerfully enough when
co-opted into *The Napoleon of Notting Hill*, but on another occasion he and G.K.C. engaged in something more like a col-
laboration. In 1909 the caricaturist Francis Carruthers Gould
(some thirty years senior to his two young friends – and han-
dled rather unkindly in *More*) drew a sketch of himself playing
the flute. Max "(after F.C.G.)" then drew his dapper self in the
same album, also tootling a flute, and G.K.C. on the back of
the Gould drawing completed what he called "the Great Flute
Series," showing himself as wildly undapper and blowing his
flute to kingdom come. It must have been quite a lark. Again,
in 1919, they contributed prefatory notes, G.K.C. "About the
Poems" and Max "About the Drawings," to Captain Lance
Sieveking's *Dressing Gowns and Glue*, with illustrations by
John Nash, but neither has anything particularly memorable
to say.[103]

Here is perhaps the place to mention two eerie train rides,
for all we know quite independent of each other – Max's "A
Memory of the Midnight Express" (1902) and G.K.C.'s "The
Secret of a Train" (1905). Max is alarmed to find himself alone
in a railway carriage on an overnight train with a sinister look-

ing man. He becomes more and more apprehensive until at last they speak: the man is a traveller in lace and has a little girl who is "pretty as a pink," whereupon Max rejoices, in Chestertonian manner, at his companion's commonplaceness and their common humanity. G.K.C. in a similar story-essay waits on a deserted railway platform; at length a mysterious darkened train makes an unscheduled stop. He gets in. The only other passenger, the guard explains, without explaining, is a dead man, whereupon G.K.C. throws away his lighted cigar, from some deep primitive impulse of piety.[104]

From time to time they can thus be on the same wavelength as imaginative writers. Max's story of "Maltby and Braxton" (1917) puts one in mind of the contrasting pairs that figure so largely in Chesterton's fiction – Auberon Quin and Adam Wayne, the satirist and the fanatic, but also the Catholic and the Rationalist in *The Ball and the Cross*, and the Tory Englishman and the radical Irishman in *The Flying Inn*. G.K.C. was aware of such polarities as early as his *Browning* when he saw the opposition of Pym and Strafford as almost an alliance. It is fanciful to relate the seven anarchists as seven days of the week in *Thursday* to Max's *Seven Men*, yet both books are highly fanciful and encourage that sort of thing: one toys with the idea before putting it back. Nevertheless, I forge ahead and brazen out the contrasts and fitting-in that I am engaged in here as I set G.K.C. and Max on a tandem bicycle, first one steering, then the other.[105] The tandem bicycle belongs unforgettably to the early twentieth century, their Fleet-Street years when they were closest. How droll would be the imagined spectacle of the two startlingly contrasting figures exchanging positions and remarks.

If they sometimes concur in imagination, they much more often concur in judgment. As we have noticed, even before their meeting G.K.C. read and commented on Max's dramatic criticism and (as I think) sided with him rather than with the heavily frivolous Clement Scott. In 1906 he includes "even

Mr. Beerbohm" among the serious critics who call for serious realistic drama; and in 1908, with a fine display of comic indignation, he attacks the "period of coarse flippancy and crude mercantile hypocrisy in the English stage which necessitated the rise of and rebuke of men rootedly and bitterly serious – like Mr. Bernard Shaw and Mr. Max Beerbohm. "Such Puritan spirits often do the work of God, if mainly in the spreading of doubt, which is the spreading of devastation." In the following year he recalled that "Mr. Max Beerbohm once maintained that playgoers should go to the theatre as communicants go to church, in the early morning," and later that year (and not long before Max to everyone's surprise withdrew to Rapallo) he notices with concern a less militant tone in his reviews:

> ... the dramatic critics, even those like Mr. Max Beerbohm, whom I both like and admire, have altogether surrendered the attempt to lead the human march. They merely walk in the other direction. It is not the nature of Man but the nature of Max that is expressed.

This last observation seems to be a reply to an almost concurrent remark of Max's:

> I think that even Mr. Chesterton, if he were a seasoned dramatic critic, would find his faith in democracy somewhat shaken. In me, certainly, the theatre has destroyed utterly such belief as I may have had in the political wisdom of the people.

– proving again, incidentally, that Max read G.K.C.[106]

We recall that Shaw repeatedly tried to persuade Chesterton to write plays. It may be noted that Max expressed the similar wish that theatrical managers might try for something above the present level of Christmas Pantomime: "Why does not one of them 'approach' Mr. Chesterton, for example? I can imagine, as the result, an admirable riot of fantasy and fun and poetry." Yes, and if he could carry it over from his fiction, there would be great, big, exhilarating, preposterous transformation scenes, to make young audiences (not to mention their parents and guardians) crow with delight.[107]

Some further concurrences of judgment, notable ones since they concern figures and topics of high importance to both. Max's remark that "Whistler really regarded Whistler as his greatest work of art" strikes G.K.C. as one of his "extraordinarily sensible and sincere critiques; he matches it in perspicacity, speaking of Whistler as "pretending to dance with levity when you are really dancing with rage." These are early; as late as *Irish Impressions* (1919) he admits to learning from Max something of moment about their shared, lifelong preoccupation, Bernard Shaw:

> But I think it is true, as Mr. Max Beerbohm once suggested to me in connection with Mr. Shaw himself, that there is a residual perversity in the Irishman, which comes after and not before the analysis of a question. There is at the last moment a cold impatience in the intellect, an irony which returns on itself and rends itself; the subtlety of a suicide.

They share – Max first, then G.K.C. – an insight not only into Shaw but into such Irishmen as J.M. Synge and Stephen Dedalus, Flann O'Brien and Samuel Beckett. Max, of course, might have observed this quality in the Irish intellectual, Michael Moon, in *Manalive* (1912).[108]

Let us, briefly, hear them on a greatly worked-over theme. Max observes:

> Women excel men in quickness and certainty of insight into the little recesses of human character, and in quickness and certainty of observation of the fine shades on the surface – observation of manners, in fact. Where women falter is in

the construction of frames for large themes, in the handling
of broad motives, in profound thinking, and so forth.

In other words, they would make good caricaturists and essayists but would be likely to fail in constructing an elaborate
plot based on an elusive idea – like *The Mirror of the Past*, shall
we say? Max quietly ranges himself with the women and sets
no very high value on "profound thinking, and so forth." Now
G.K.C.

> Mr. Max Beerbohm, I see, remarked the other day that in
> his opinion women were unable intellectually to create or
> achieve. I think it is quite a mistake to put it on this intellec-
> tual ground; it is a little supercilious, and it is to a great ex-
> tent untrue. Women are as intellectual as the Devil in their
> own way. The real difference is not intellectual, but moral
> – they lack camaraderie. There they stand on this issue and
> there we leave them.[109]

As well as thinking *with* Max, Chesterton (as we have already seen several times) thought *about* him – even worried
about him a little. The contrast he builds, in *Heretics* (1905),
between the "humane aetheticism" of Max and the "cruel aestheticism" of William Ernest Henley, the journalist and poet
of a highly aggressive imperialism, though left undeveloped,
must seem to us applicable late in recent time to the "humane"
flower people and the "cruel" heavy-metal types, allowing of
course for a drastic falling-off in intelligence. In the same year
he wrote this:

> Mr. Max Beerbohm in one of his most delightful and ab-
> surd essays has denounced the fire brigade as a band of van-
> dals who destroy a "fair thing." He has threatened to start an
> opposition fire brigade whose pipes shall be filled not with
> water but with oil. Nero was only Max made serious; Nero

was only Max without his good nature; Nero was only Max in action.

There is much virtue in that "only." And Chesterton seems not to have noticed how deftly Max had anticipated this criticism in the very essay in question:

> I am far from exalting arson to the level of a fine art. Nothing is easier than to be an incendiary. All you want is a box of matches and a sense of beauty. I know, too, that fires have often been made for unworthy ends, for the gratification of revenge or, even, personal vanity. Nero set light to Rome that he might divert the ears of the musical critics from his indifferent fiddling....[110]

Chesterton had the good sense to treat Max, not as a "heretic," like Shaw or Wells or Kipling, but as a writer in the comic mode. He observed about wits like Whistler and humorists like Max – "whose humour was so dainty and delicate as to become a kind of topsy-turvy transcendentalism" – that "these great wits and great humourists had one genuine defect – they could not laugh." I am very much afraid that by laugh he meant belly-laugh. This deserves a full answer. Perpend.[111]

The belly-laugh. Scorn it not. This life affords a few, but only a few, better things. G.K.C. seems to occupy this bailiwick easily. Just look at him and look at Max. But Hobgoblin must not be allowed to run away with the garland from Apollo. He was the man for the pub and enjoyed popular jollifications; but unlike the elegant Max, unlike the fragile Arthur Symons, unlike the bankerly T.S. Eliot, he indulged no cult of the music hall and seemed seldom to have entered that temple of "the vulgarity of the people." To be sure, Max in youth posed as an "earnest student of music halls" (that word *earnest* again!), and as a good Meredithian wore a feasting smile therein, and even as we have noticed, in a desperate stylistic gamble praised the "hard gemlike flame" of their gaslight, but one does not sustain such a taste without some native aptitude for vulgarity. And as an old man he goes so far as to sing music-hall songs on the radio, including one of his own composition, becoming thereby as popular a media personality as Chesterton might have been if he had lived longer.[112]

Max had written "The Humour of the Public" as early as 1902, our point of inception. In this essay he animadverts upon the lack of a sense of humour: "to convict a man of that lack is to strike him with one blow to the level of the beasts of the field.... A man will admit cheerfully that he does not know one tune from another, or that he cannot discern the vintages of wines.... But I have never heard a man assert that he has no sense of humour." Max continues: "Having no love for the public, I have often accused that body of having no sense of humour" – an imputation he wishes now ostensibly to reject, really to restate. The public likes humour in likely places, the private person (such as himself and his reader) in unlikely. From long frequentation of the music hall and from short but intense perusal of comic papers he draws up a list of some fourteen stereotypes that put the public in the frame to laugh.[113]

This piece by Max made a strong impression on Chesterton. The disquisition on humour by Auberon Quin early in *The Napoleon of Notting Hill* derives directly from it:

> "If," said Mr. Quin, "I were to say that you did not see the great truths of science exhibited by that tree, though they stared any man of intellect in the face, what would you think or say? You would merely regard me as a pedant with some unimportant theory about vegetable cells. If I were to say that you did not see in that tree the vile mismanagement of local politics, you would dismiss me as a socialist crank with some particular fad about public parks. If I were to say that you were guilty of the supreme blasphemy of looking at that tree and not seeing in it a new religion, a special

revelation of God, you would simply say I was a mystic, and think no more about me. But if" – and he lifted a pontifical hand – "if I say that you cannot see the humour of that tree, and that I see the humour of it – my God! you will roll about at my feet.

He paused a moment, and then resumed.

"Yes; a sense of humour, a weird and delicate sense of humour, is the new religion of mankind! It is towards that men will strain themselves with the asceticism of saints.

"Exercises, spiritual exercises, will be set in it."

This is close to Max's argument, idiom, and style, though the examples Auberon Quin will give are, strictly, not humour but nonsense.[114]

Chesterton returns to the subject of humour and the question of Max in the essay on "Cockneys and their Jokes" (1906):

I remember that Mr. Max Beerbohm (who has every merit except democracy) attempted to analyse the jokes at which the mob laughs. He divided them into three sections: jokes about bodily humiliation, jokes about things alien, such as foreigners, and jokes about bad cheese. Mr. Max Beerbohm thought he understood the first two forms; but I am not so sure that he did. In order to understand vulgar humour it is not enough to be humorous. One must also be vulgar, as I am.

(Of Max's fourteen divisions, we notice that G.K.C., who always quoted from memory, remembered only three.) In his theatrical review, under the title "Tickled Groundlings" (1908), Max raised the question again apropos of the tendency of audiences to laugh at a kiss or an embrace on the stage:

In a recent essay Mr. Chesterton chid me for lack of sympathy with the humour of the multitude. He wished me democratic enough to see the point of jokes about bad cheese, mothers-in-law, and other traditional themes; and he eloquently insisted that in all such jokes there was a grand spiritual significance. I have no doubt there is.

But he has every doubt about the laughability of the last embrace of two young tragic lovers. He continues:

> I should, of course, be able to join in the general merriment if the actor and actress impersonating the lovers did not rise to the solemnity of the occasion. I should laugh if they exchanged a resounding kiss, or if, in excess of energy, they lost their balance and rolled over. I assure Mr. Chesterton I am quite democratic enough for that.

The matter lodged in his mind, or stuck in his craw, for he returned to it again after a year, conceding G.K.C.'s main point, about democracy:

> Mr. Chesterton once chid me, in a brilliant essay, for not cherishing in my heart the ideal of democracy. It is quite true that I don't believe at all firmly in (what has always been to Mr. Chesterton a dark and mystical reality) the wisdom of the people. I would not stake sixpence on the people's capacity for governing itself, and not a penny on its capacity for governing me.

So there. On the subject of the humour of the people, both are humorous, neither is out of humour.[115]

Now, as for laughter, G.K.C. has always been justly famous for rollicking, but we must not forget that, on scarcer occasions, Max can rollick too. Two very boyish young men, Will Rothenstein and Max Beerbohm, one convivial evening thought it a good idea to ring doorbells and run away – into the arms of a police constable. Max's essay on "Laughter" (1920), which begins by sporting with Henri Bergson's solemn treatment of the same subject, goes on to recount, contagiously, Dr. Johnson's merriment at the expense of an earnest gentleman who told the gathering that he had just drawn up his will – the "Testator" Johnson called him, a term accurate and somehow absurd:

> He had created gloriously much out of nothing at all. There he sat, old and ailing and unencouraged by the company, but soaring higher and higher in absurdity, more and more rejoicing, and still soaring and rejoicing after he had gone out into the night with Boswell, till at last in Fleet Street his paroxysms were too much for him and he could no more.

How readily accessible that Fleet Street would be to the imagination and memory of Max or G.K.C. Max then goes on to recount another instance of "extreme laughter," from Tom Moore's memoir of Byron. Visiting Samuel Rogers, whom they both venerated as the greatest of living poets – dignified, elderly, a stockbroker, rich – they happen upon a presentation copy of *Poems on Several Occasions* by Lord Thurloe. Not a word of Max's paragraph must be missed:

> The two young poets found in this elder's Muse much that was so execrable as to be delightful. They were soon, as they turned the pages, held in throes of laughter, laughter that was but intensified by the endeavours of their correct and nettled host to point out the genuine merits of his friend's work. And then suddenly – oh joy! – "we lighted," Moore records, "on the discovery that our host, in addition to his sincere approbation of some of this book's contents, had also the motive of gratitude for standing by its author, as one of the poems was a warm and, I need not add, well-deserved panegyric on himself. We were, however" – the narrative has an added charm from Tom Moore's demure care not

to offend the still-living Rogers – "too far gone in nonsense for even this eulogy, in which we both so heartily agreed, to stop us." The opening line of the poem was, as well as I can recollect, "When Rogers o'er this labour bent;" and Lord Byron undertook to read it aloud; – but he found it impossible to get beyond the first two words. Our laughter had now increased to such a pitch that nothing could restrain it. Two or three times he began; but no sooner had the words "When Rogers" passed his lips, than our fit burst out afresh, – till even Mr. Rogers himself, with all his feeling for our injustice, found it impossible not to join in; and we were, at last, all three in such a state of inextinguishable laughter, that, had the author himself been of our party, I question much whether he could, have resisted the infection." The final fall and dissolution of Rogers, Rogers behaving as badly as either of them, is all that was needed to give perfection to this heart-warming scene.

Tom Moore and Max collaborate in telling it well, with Chestertonian gusto. How sober in contrast is G.K.C.'s article on Byron and Moore, which is preoccupied with their moral character and does not remember and embrace them as laughers.[116]

If Max can once or twice be expansive and Chestertonian, G.K.C. can be witty and ironic and Maximilian, as we have seen in many passages of *The Napoleon of Notting Hill*. One other example. His profound fear and distrust of the Nineties ethos wanes in his later writings, most notably is this high-spirited defence of the somewhat conventionally Bohemian unconventionality of Robert Louis Stevenson as displayed in his dress and manner. Before I quote it, let us remind ourselves of the memorable "Compare me!" passage in Max's letter to Bohun Lynch and, lying behind both, the passage where Thackeray imagines the perfect Roundabout Paper:

It was to have contained all the deep pathos of Addison; the logical precision of Rabelais; the childlike playfulness of Swift; the manly stoicism of Sterne; the metaphysical depth of Goldsmith; the blushing modesty of Fielding; the epigrammatic terseness of Walter Scott; the uproarious humour of Sam Richardson; and the gay simplicity of Sam Johnson....

Chesterton on Stevenson gets into the swing of this, coming as close to Thackeray as Max ever did, and that is close indeed:

Everybody seems to assume that among the artists of his time he was entirely alone in his affectation. Contrasting in this respect with the humdrum respectability of Oscar Wilde, notable as the very reverse of the evangelical meekness of Jimmy Whistler, standing out as he does against the stodgy chapel-going piety of Max Beerbohm, having none of the cheery commonplaces of Aubrey Beardsley or the prosaic self-effacement of Richard Le Gallienne, he naturally aroused attention by the slightest deviation into oddity or dandyism; things notoriously unpopular among the decadents of the 'nineties.[117]

Much as Chesterton enjoyed first complimenting, then engaging with, even sparring with, Max, they cannot really be regarded as rival essayists. Though he wrote hundreds, Chesterton often refers to the familiar essay in a tone of disparagement or estrangement, most clearly in "An Apology for Buffoons" (1928), where (quoting Father Ronald Knox) he distinguishes writers who say "I believe" from writers who murmur "one does feel" – the latter being the more egotistical because they assume that their readers will be interested not in the subject under discussion but in the personality of the essayist. "All my articles are articles and ... none of my articles are essays," he roundly asserts, and goes on to parody a vacuous though "light and delicate" essay, belonging in the hemisphere though not in the neighbourhood of Max. (Max quite nicely dissociates himself from the worst case of the essayist, the essayist who obviously touts for our affection). Chesterton's sort of writer, and Shaw's too, and yes, the raucous Mencken's, "deals with big things noisily and the other with small things quietly. But there is more of the note of superiority in the man who always treats of things smaller than himself than the man who always treats of things greater than himself." Having owned to the charge of being something of a demagogue and something of a buffoon, he concludes thus:

> I do not really mean, of course, that the essayist is an egoist in any selfish sense. Nobody in the world, I imagine, gets more good than I do out of good essays like those of Mr. Max Beerbohm or Mr. E.V. Lucas or Mr. Robert Lynd. I only ask, in all seriousness, that they should understand the necessities of our sort of self-assertion as well as recognizing the existence of their own. And I do ask them to believe that when we try to make our sermons and speeches more or less amusing, it is for the very simple and even modest reason that we do not see why the audience should listen unless it is more or less amused. Our mode of speech is conditioned by the fact that it really is what some have fancifully supposed the function of speech to be; something addressed by somebody to somebody else. It has of necessity all the vices and vulgarities attaching to a speech that really is a speech and not a soliloquy.

So Chesterton holds his own.[118]

Max might well reply to the latent charge of unseriousness that his own adherence to the Horatian *respice finem* – know how you are going to end before you start – is a form of seriousness and a compliment to the seriousness of the reader's attention to details of expression, and that in this regard he is more serious than G.K.C. the improviser.[119]

They are, of course – to disallow G.K.C.'s disclaimer – both essayists. Both stand in the great, the undulating and diverse, tradition of Montaigne. Both take an idea and (no, do not run it into the ground) handle it until it bends and becomes pliant in their hands; both combine genuine enquiry with a controlled sense of humour; and the personality of each is signed on every page. To continue a rapid placing of each in the tradition of the essay: Max, like Bacon, loves the arresting sentence and can, with controlled incongruity, even quote Bacon on royalty in his own very different essay on the subject; from Lamb he takes a reminiscent habit and a touch (much drier in Max) of self-depreciation and self-appreciation; from Thackeray, a pleasant and ironic style with the appearance more of ease than of effort; from Pater, smoothness, the enamelled surface, exactitude of syntax; like Oscar Wilde as described by Pater, "he always has a phrase," and is friendly and desirous of pleasing; from Stevenson, the urge to "play the sedulous ape"; from Chesterton, on occasion, the use of the *argumentum ad absurdum*. So too with G.K.C. With Samuel Johnson he shares weight and moral seriousness and the power (less often the desire) to crush; from Cobbett, audacity in his attack on the whole Whig thing; from Wilde, primarily and indubitably his reliance on paradox and the inverted truism; from Nietzsche the moral aphorism and from the captioned paragraphs of Bernard Shaw's prefaces, his alacrity of spirits and the continual sense of a new beginning.[120]

CHAPTER SIX

Parody and Caricature

If Max's satire is, in Oscar Wilde's phrase, a "silver dagger," G.K.C. can swinge his sword-stick impressively, especially when draped in a cape. There is something playful about both weapons, and while Chesterton used absent-mindedly to lunge and parry with his sword just as he often made the sign of the cross with his cigar, both of these gentle, good-humoured men refrained, most of the time, from using them to stab or bludgeon their adversaries.[121]

Most of the time, not all. Once, Chesterton let the sun go down on his wrath, with a vengeance. After the death of his brother Cecil in the Great War, he wrote and published an open letter to Rufus Isaacs, Lord Reading, whose brother had escaped prosecution in the Marconi Scandal, which Cecil had done much to uncover. The letter is so dreadful, so carefully penned, so murderous, that one trembles for the writer. Having no such personal animus, Max's well-aimed cartoon (to be discussed shortly) is blandness itself. Some of Max's political cartoons, however, strike one as fierce and out of character, G.K.C. himself noting in 1921 that Max "has lately been less successful in making fun of labour than he has always been in making fun of luxury." Most of the decorated and "improved" books in Max's library (which include many presentation copies) are good fun, but some show a prolonged and meticulous hostility. Nothing is done to the glory of God – nothing to compare to the splendid illuminated cross on the ballot in *The*

Return of Don Quixote,[122] which the enumerators rejected as "spoiled."

Max wields his weapon even when most he appears a mild essayist. In the very early Letter to *The Yellow Book* (1894) he concentrated the defence of his essay on cosmetics in a supremely offensive comma: "It is a pity that critics should show so little sympathy with writers, and curious when we consider that most of them tried to be writers themselves, once." Max proved to have that prime qualification of a good theatrical critic, unkindness, so that his quite frequent words of praise and encouragement were never dulled by the fuggy atmosphere of too easy approbation. The prolonged tussle with Clement Scott (that we and G.K.C. have already looked at) ended with victory for Max and the flight of the adversary. Poor Arthur Wing Pinero can never have fully recovered from the examination, the dissection, the vivisection of his style, and Max administers a well-deserved spanking to a self-advertising American, J.G. Huneker, having first pretended to think him a juvenile. Metaphorically at least, he kicks Jerome K. Jerome down three flights of stairs and then with schoolboy fiendishness reveals his middle name (Klapka). Max's indignant dismissal of Jerome's play, *The Passing of the Third Floor Back* (where at the final curtain a nameless, soupy-supernatural figure, challenged to reveal himself, simply extends his arms) is final – so corrosive indeed that it seeps through to, and devours, the little soft spot at the conclusion of *The Man Who Was Thursday*, when Sunday, similarly challenged, asks "Can ye drink of the cup that I drink of?" Chesterton deals with the matter much more mildly when he suggests, apropos of the play, that telling people how good they are may be the best method for "suicidal outcasts whose moral backs are broken" but unrealistic and sentimental for the proud and self-satisfied. (In fairness to Jerome it should be noted that his low horse, *Three Men in a Boat* is a much better animal than his high horse, *Third Floor Back*.)[123]

Max's lifelong rejection of Rudyard Kipling amounted almost to a vendetta, and it is interesting to note that he and G.K.C. both found something feminine in Kipling's excessive *machismo*. The real Kipling, who had a vision and a dream, is invisible to Max and to G.K.C. alike. On the other hand, Max deplored the insipidity of Alice Meynell, a very nice person, quietly applauded in her day for her literary thoughts, in a review and a parody (neither reprinted) and, without naming her, in his essay on Ouida. He was, however, not merely on balance but predominantly, like Oscar Wilde and unlike Whistler, the sort of wit who would rather keep his friend and lose his jest than keep his jest and lose his friend. He certainly did keep his friends, and while some, like Chesterton, were easy to hold onto, others, like Belloc, could be combative to the point of orneriness. He exclaimed to S.N. Behrman about the two of them, "They had their blind spots, but they were delightful men. Such enormous gusto, you know, such gaiety, and feeling for life." And the liking was reciprocal. The Chestertons enjoyed a happy visit with the Beerbohms in Rapallo; and Evelyn Waugh (himself a crusty character) recalling with affection the generosity of Max, recalls also "how joyously Belloc and Baring acclaimed him!" That is how most (not all) of the subjects of his parodies, the victims of his caricatures, regarded Max.[124]

Essayists from beginning to end, writers of fiction from time to time, our authors proceed in tandem; but when parody and caricature are mentioned, it is Max's name that springs to mind, as Chesterton's does not. Yet it may point up the supremacy of the one in these fields if we recall the solid achievement of the other.

G.K. Chesterton: parodist. We have already looked at the parodies in *Napoleon* – of the bucolic and the urban poems and their review in the high court of literary journalism, and of the attempt at war reporting in various prose styles, each one more comically askew. His "Variations on an Air" (1932), "composed on having to appear in a pageant as Old King Cole," earns a place in Dwight Macdonald's classic collection of *Parodies*. In it, Tennyson, Browning, Yeats, Swinburne, and Whitman all amplify the nursery rhyme in their own styles. Here is how the young Yeats observes that Old King Cole was a merry old soul:

> Of an old King in a story
>   From the grey sea-folk I have heard,
> Whose heart was no more broken
>   Than the wings of a bird.

This little sequence is a *jeu d'esprit*, an exception among his verses and quite exceptionally good. What is the rule in his prose writing is a sort of running parody, showing itself when he gives the ideas and often the style of his opponent a twist of exaggeration (characteristically introduced by "it is as if"), so that the whole scene is transformed. *Reductio ad absurdum* is a parodic device.[125]

G.K. Chesterton: caricaturist and satiric draftsman. This is an aspect of his work ignored by Max and largely forgotten by his large continuing public. This may seem strange because G.K.C. "took art," as Max never did. His lifelong friend, E.C. Bentley, observed that he learned no tricks at the Slade School, nothing that he did not already know. The French critic Christiane D'Haussey, went to the trouble to write a letter of enquiry to the School and received this reply: "The only information that our records reveal is that he attended the Slade from 1893 to 1895. There is no note that he received any diploma or certificate, nor that he completed a course." He seems not to have impressed anyone or to have equipped himself for a life in art, or commercial art, or the teaching of art.[126]

Nevertheless, he did possess, from very early days, a knack of humorous illustration, like Edward Lear before him and James Thurber after – the Lear who matched goofy poem with goofy drawing, not the highly accomplished landscape watercolourist. Bentley's *Biography for Beginners* appeared in 1905, with 29 drawings by Chesterton to accompany the clerihews, the earliest of which go back to their school days, to 1890. One of these, on John Stuart Mill, we have looked at; another, on the German-born South African millionaire, Alfred Beit, is the earliest attack on the Jewish capitalist-imperialist, a theme that must soon be considered; a third, on Hilaire Belloc, is amusing not so much for itself as because in pose and features the Belloc figure serves as a model for a boisterous upper-class twister (strongly suspected of pulling a horse in a race) in *The Emerald of Catherine the Great* (1926), a quarter of a century later, a long time to cherish a joke.[127]

The comic drawings in *Graybeards at Play* (1900), his earliest book of nonsense verse, resemble those of the clerihews – economical, sure, fantastic, exclamatory, for the figures encourage us to supply some risible sound ranging in decibels from bang to simper. Only one other of his own books (except the posthumous collection, *The Coloured Lands*) features his drawings. This is the set of stories, *The Club of Queer Trades* (1905), which has no fewer than 32 illustrations. Here again the farcical energy jumps off the page, and here again the young Belloc appears, in the character of Basil Grant stripping an impostor of his farcical clergyman's whiskers or rising to his feet amid a surge of song and cheers. This by the way is one of very few likenesses that I have found in his drawings (except of himself): there is little of the cartoonist's cult of personality, as compared to Max, who gives us a whole National Comic Portrait Gallery of Public figures.[128]

It is strange, and unexplained, that Chesterton should have provided no more illustrations to his own works of fiction after this spirited first outing. It is all the more strange that he should be the regular illustrator of the fiction of Belloc. His name appears on the dust jacket with the author's, and in some cases the book is advertised as "the new Chesterbelloc." Belloc related how they worked together, Chesterton's sketch sometimes pointing the way for characterization and plot:

He would, with a soft pencil capable of giv[ing] every gra-
dation an emphasis from the lightest touch to the dead
black point and line, set down, in gestures that were like
caresses sometime, sometime like commands, sometimes
like rapier-thrusts, the whole of what a man or woman was,
and he would get the thing down on paper with the rapidity
that only comes from complete possession.

Of Belloc's seventeen books of fiction, ten are illustrated by
Chesterton. These range from *Emmanuel Burden* (1904, the
year of *Napoleon*) to *The Hedge and the Horse* (1936, the year of
G.K.C.'s death). There are, by my count, over 270 drawings,
most of them sharply observed, satirical catchings of character
in action. Of these, nineteen have Jewish subjects. That is to
say, slightly less than one in fourteen, an appreciable minority
not large enough to be an obsession but large enough to be a
problem.[129]

Somewhere in any treatment of Chesterton in his relation
to Belloc the candid observer must face what they would call
the "Jewish question." Neither had any time for pseudo-scien-
tific racial doctrines (at a time when such notions had some
respectability and were rife in the most surprising circles):
they very specifically scorned the idea of Jewish blood, Teu-
tonic natural supremacy or Anglo-Saxon blood-ties. However,
they recognized in the Jew, as they recognized in the Muslim,
not semitic blood but a culture and a religion which they saw
to be foreign to Europe. Jews and Muslims are not Catholic
Christians, as Europeans ought to be; it seemed as simple as
that. It is not so for us. Today, three-quarters of a century after
the end of the Second World War, when the barbarities of the
Nazis were thoroughly exposed and, one had hoped, effectively
condemned, antisemitism is again on the rise in Europe, Great
Britain, and the Americas, as is hatred of persons, especially
immigrants, who seem in any way culturally different. We now
understand that any strong desire for cultural and religious

homogeneity entails antisemitism and other forms of cruel prejudice. The context of Belloc's fiction and Chesterton's illustrations is the right place for their antisemitism to be raised.[130]

Hilaire Belloc's best friend and worst enemy can agree that he was not bound by ordinary good manners or common decency, even by the standards of his own comparatively free and easy age. He intended readers of his brisk, ironic political novels to enjoy a guilty indulgence in the soft porn of prejudice and the harder stuff of hate. Many of them are set in what was his future and is now our past, a time when the Prime Minister of Great Britain is a woman and the two major parties are Communists on the right and Anarchists on the left. His harping on the Jewish practice of taking non-Jewish surnames or titles becomes something of an obsession, as when "Mr. Montague", a pawnbroker, is hailed as the bearer of the old crusading name. This is intended to be funny. In his book on *The Jews*, Belloc does for once concede that their surnames were required and assigned only at the time of the Napoleonic emancipation and hence do not usually have deep familial or religious meaning for their bearers, a point he usually finds it inconvenient to remember. There is something disingenuous, not to say immoral, about this whole matter: he, and Chesterton when in this vein, do not see fit to recall that an Irish clergyman named Prunty renamed himself "Brontë," as redolent of something finer. They both knew and admired a Pole named (that is, baptized) Josef Teodor Konrad Walecz Korzeniowski, who had served in the British Merchant Marine, had written novels under the plausible English name Joseph Conrad, and had settled in Kent to live the life of an English gentleman, though retaining a strong affiliation with Polish aristocracy to the end. Woe betide him at Chesterton's or Belloc hands if he had been Jewish.[131]

No, that is too strong. What they take their stand against more broadly, although it unfortunately includes antisemitism, is the hagiography of capitalism, whether the over-powerful and over-rewarded tycoon be a Jewish financier in the tradition of the Rothschilds, Alfred Beit, Alfred Mond, or an American Robber Baron, or one of the Press Lords who, under such titles as Lord Toronto or Lord Winnipeg, are for them stereotypes of the worst sort of pushing vulgarian colonial. And in novel after novel, the hold these various operators achieve over solid British types, through usury, bribery, news management, manipulation of the market – including the art market and the academic market – is due to a combination of slackness, self-indulgence and cupidity on the part of the victim. Belloc, who as a prolific writer lived by his wits, has more admiration for the scoundrel who lives by his wits than for the layabout who fails to do so.[132]

Of the satiric novels of Belloc illustrated by Chesterton, the first, *Emmanuel Burden* (1904), and the penultimate, *The Postmaster General* (1932), may detain us for a moment. The former is the most overtly hostile to Jews; the latter has a Jewish leading character who is both admirable and convincing. *Emmanuel Burden*, written ironically in the style of a pious Victorian biography, is essentially an account, perceptible and dismaying to the reader but not to the smooth conventional biographer, of the destruction of the old upright entrepreneurial world of business and trade by a newer, impersonal world of imperial exploitation and financial speculation. But is it impersonal? This new, corrupt order finds mainly Jewish agents, a young efficient fixer and reliever of financial embarrassments, Mr. Harbury, and an age-old, reptilian imperial financier, Mr. Barnett, later Lord Lambeth, who will appear still later in other novels as the Duke of Battersea. Four of Chesterton's 34 drawings are devoted to these and will immediately be identified today as vicious stereotypes. They passed in their time as merely humorous, and so much the worse for their time. In my judgment the best Chesterton drawings are in *Emmanuel Burden* – not only the ones mentioned but those of Burden himself and his wife and son, and of Lord Benthorpe, so aristocratic, so plausible, so weak.

Now and then Chesterton and Belloc distinguish between the bulk of ordinary, hard-working, mainly poor Jews and the few conspicuous players of the market – the financial, academic, and art market. This distinction is easy enough to make, as it is for the unthinking Gentile to despise poor Jews but to make self-congratulatory exceptions for the few with undeniable talents or great wealth or usefulness to one's career. Chesterton's Zionist sympathies and, what is more important, his stern and consistent condemnation of the whole Nazi movement from the beginning, make his use of this distinction believable, until we remember his "flippant fancy" arguing that the Jews should have a homeland of their own so they can get out of Europe and stop changing their names and adopting European dress. What about Belloc? His considered, if deplorable opinion, as distinct from his automatic prejudices, is spelled out in his book on *The Jews* (1922): it is essentially that of French Tridentine Roman Catholicism. But in *The Postmaster General* the elderly, harmless politician of the title, Wilfred Halterton, no scoundrel but anxious to leave politics with his livelihood ensured by an appointment to the board room, enters into the usual sort of arrangement involving conflict of interest and falls into the hands first of a cunning capitalist and then of a wily Home Secretary (a former labour leader), who are indeed scoundrels. Years before, he had without fault run over and injured a young Jewish boy and, instead of merely apologizing or paying, had shown real human concern and sympathy and had thereby won the heart of the boy's elder brother, whose experience of Gentiles had been formed in the pogroms that drove his family from their native Russia. Belloc's account of a pogrom is strongly written and blazes with indignation. The boy becomes a Cambridge mathematician and the brother a financier, both single-minded achievers in their fields, and they and the Postmaster General maintain friendly relations. It is the older brother, the picture of integrity and effectiveness, who steps in with the knowledge and the will to foil and vex the two twisters.[133]

Before we leave this subject, something should be said about Max. Because of his foreign-sounding name, Max Beerbohm often encountered the assumption that he was of Jewish origin. Whether it was intended as praise or not, he corrected it calmly. His two closest lifelong friends, Will Rothenstein and Reggie Turner, were Jewish, as was his wife, Florence Kahn. Max adopted a pose of comic anti-Americanism to tease her, but never struck a pose, comic or otherwise, evoking jewish stereotypes. Nonetheless, an observer of his satiric drawings will not unreasonably interpret two of his *Fifty Caricatures* (1913) as abusive of Jews. One of them, early in the reign of King George the Fifth, has the caption "Are we as welcome as ever?" Shown are five well-known figures from the late King Edward the Seventh's inner circle, all financiers, all immensely rich, all in profile trumpeting their Jewishness. The other has the caption "Some Ministers of the Crown, who (monstrous though it seem) have severally some spare pounds to invest, implore Sir Rufus Isaacs to tell them if he knows of any stocks which they could buy without fear of ultimate profit." This of course is in reference to the Marconi Scandal that so exercised Cecil Chesterton and Belloc and through them G. K. Chesterton himself.[134]

Now it is time to look at Max's caricatures, specifically those of G.K.C. There are eight of Chesterton alone and a further ten in which he figures along with others, few or many. The earliest of the solo pictures (1904) shows "Mr. G.K. Chesterton giving the world a kiss." Gilbert and Frances went to see it in the Carfax Gallery, and she wrote in her diary, "It's more like Thackeray, very funny though." Perceptive of her: Max, who could answer "adsum" along with Colonel Newcome and Thackeray himself to the roll-call of the Charterhouse School, was a lifelong Thackerayan (as G.K.C. was a lifelong Dickensian), and the pose here is very similar to the familiar sketch, in the National Portrait Gallery, of the near-sighted Thackeray holding a book close to his face.[135]

Max returned to G.K.C. in 1907 and 1911; and in 1912 he drew the celebrated caricature of Chesterton giving an after-dinner speech, cigar in hand, his shirt showing under his waistcoat like a sort of equator, his girth a whole terrestrial globe. Chesterton was right in noticing that Max's art can be stylized and abstract to the borders of geometry. Another sketch and a drawing, undated, show him full-length, gesticulating, in evening dress – variations on the time-honoured theme; but in the remaining caricatures G.K.C. shares the space with other persons. Some of these are large assemblies or deputations, such as the one where Max's subjects, or victims, formally beg him to "give over," an antique form of "lay off." G.K.C. here is planted at the back, being so bulky and so tall.[136]

Bernard Shaw is by a very wide margin Max's favourite literary subject. In *Heretics* (1905) G.K.C. had conceded Shaw's consistency and that he was not standing on his head. In *Fifty Caricatures* (1913) Max takes this up, conceding again the consistency but not the conventional stance: placing himself in the picture, he expresses the "mild surprise of one who, revisiting England after long absence, finds that the dear fellow has not moved." There is Shaw, standing on his head, his legs crossed in a gesture of nonchalance. I wonder if anyone has noticed that Shaw's posture is very like that of the Hanged Man in the Tarot card?[137]

In two earlier caricatures, both of 1909, Shaw had shared the page with Chesterton. Of the two, "Leaders of Thought" is an encounter of sphere and tangent and not much more. Much more is "Mr. Shaw's Sortie," showing a globular, belted G.K.C. behind a wall (reminiscent in shape of Humpty Dumpty though in no peril of falling) speaking the concluding words of his new book on Shaw. In the foreground, G.B.S. twice over, in two operatic costumes – G.B.S. in a dancer's tutu, knock-kneed, carrying a spear and tooting a megaphone, and G.B.S. as Mephisto, looking the less bizarre and more reliable of the two. What are the vibrant words of peroration that accompany this harlequinade?

> "But this shall be written of our time: that when the Spirit who Denies besieged the last citadel, blaspheming life itself, there were some – there was one especially – whose voice was heard, and whose spear was not broken."

To this worked-up eloquence and gesticulating camaraderie Max all but says, *sotto voce*, "chuck it!"[138]

In 1925, as one of a set but not published with the others of the same title, he drew the encounter of "the Old and the Young Self." The Young Self is astonishingly like the photograph of Chesterton at the age of sixteen. It is not unlikely that Max may have seen it, briefly, on a visit; if so, how quickly and permanently must the impression have registered, for it is just about impossible to reconstruct imaginatively a thin youth from a fat man. The Youth says (and here again Max's ample caption is as carefully composed as the drawing):

> "Oh yes, I drank some beer only the other day, and rather liked it; and of course the Crusades were glorious. But all this about English public life being honeycombed with corruption, and about the infallibility of the Pope, and the sacramental qualities of beer, and the soul-cleansing powers of Burgundy, and the immaculate conception of France, and the determination of the Jews to enslave us, and the instant need that we should get straight back into the Middle Ages, and –"

To which the Old Self replies, "Well, you haven't met Belloc."[139]

Appearing in *A Book of Caricatures* (1907) is "Mr. Hilaire Belloc, striving to win Mr. Gilbert Chesterton over from the errors of Geneva." Short, burly Belloc stands on a chair to harangue the seated, grotesquely obese Chesterton; Belloc's tankard, full, is in his left hand; Chesterton is emptying his, the features of his face drawn into it. One questions this: G.K.C. liked his beer, there is no gainsaying, and drank a lot, but did he guzzle? He was a man who was thirsty, but he never wrote as if he had a hangover or as if all he could think about was the next drink – and he wrote hugely and all the time, often, to be sure, in pubs. Even *The Flying Inn*, a bibulous book, could not have been written by Max's guzzler. The drawing strongly implies that he would rather drink than argue; not so. Indeed, the caricature is altogether ill-aimed, for Chesterton, a liberal theist by upbringing, first a high-church Anglican and then a Roman Catholic by adult profession, at no time in his life assented to Calvinism, "the errors of Geneva."[140]

Nor is it kind, and the unkindest details are the feet. Belloc's are neat enough, but Chesterton's! We know that Max was shocked by a certain grossness about the back of Bernard Shaw's neck, but we should also take note that he had a thing about feet. In a quick poll let us observe Max's literary caricatures making, not a sign manual but a sign pedal, beginning with the famous one of Oscar Wilde speaking the name of Rossetti to an audience of earnest Americans: his feet are admirable, theirs deplorable. The elegantly shod include Lord Byron, Browning, Hardy, Whistler, Lytton Strachey, George Moore, Joseph Conrad (who is well dressed and well shod on a desert island) and of course, pre-eminently, Max himself. The clumsy-footed include Robert Burns, Walt Whitman, Ibsen, Shaw, Hauptmann, the admired Maeterlinck, the hated Kipling, the likeable Chesterton. It is no accident that the Duke's feet are praised in *Zuleika Dobson* and those of the wretched Noaks dispraised. Max is at his most world-historical and Spenglerian in the drawing expressive of "The Grave Misgivings of the Nineteenth Century and the Wicked Amusement of the Eighteenth, in Watching the Progress (or Whatever it is) of the Twentieth": the three characters have aristocratic, bourgeois, and proletarian feet. Oddly enough, Ada Chesterton, on the first page of her memoir of the family, says this of her brother-in-law:

> He was a striking figure in those days, upright and with a gallant carriage. His magnificent head had a thick mane of wavy chestnut hair, inevitably [sic] rumpled. His hands were beautifully shaped, with long slender fingers, but in sudden, almost painful contra-distinction, his feet were very small and podgy, and never seemed to afford a stable base.

Michael Asquith also recalls Chesterton's "incongruously small feet," and photographs confirm this, though the feet are seldom in the picture: head and torso are usually enough, and if he is in company, he stands at the back. It is as if Max had judged G.K.C. as the sort of person whose feet ought to be gross, and never gave them his "mild attentive gaze."[141]

Of one caricature we have only a ghostly caption. Father John O'Connor recalls a Max cartoon of Belloc and Chesterton (at the Chestertons' Battersea flat, that is, before 1908), with a special dedication in Max's hand, "... a paragraph in the Chestertonian manner to the effect that scoffing was true worship, and the Yah! of the rude boy in the street is but an act of reverence, being but the first syllable of the Unutterable Name!" I wonder where this has disappeared to.[142]

To match this ghostly caricature there is a slight puzzle or confusion about Henry James and Max's celebrated parody, "The Mote in the Middle Distance." In 1907 Chesterton took issue with James's story, "The Turn of the Screw" (1898): it was, he said, "one of the most powerful things ever written, and ... one of the things about which it is most permissible to doubt whether it ought ever to have been written at all." (It was, he might have observed, a Christmas story, told on what may have been the Feast of the Holy Innocents.) He concludes: "I will approve the thing as well as admire it if he will write another tale just as powerful about two children and Santa Claus." This, I say, is puzzling, since Max as long ago as 1896 had thought of writing a parody of James on a Christmas theme, in which all mention of Christmas would be avoided, and in the Christmas issue of the *Saturday Review*, 1906, had published a set of eight parodies, including "The Mote," which already took up G.K.C.'s challenge for James before it had been thrown down. The set also included "Christmas Day," a deft parody of Chesterton himself, and so it is just about impossible that G.K.C. should not have seen the little collection. To complicate matters further, in *The Victorian Age* (1913), remembering Max but forgetting his own challenge, G.K.C. appreciatively remarks that "only Max could imagine Henry James writing about Christmas."[143]

Fresh from writing his parody of Chesterton, Max makes a few explicit observations about the way the style of G.K.C. is the man himself. These occur in the essay, "A Morris for May-Day" (1907), which begins thus:

> Not long ago a prospectus was issued by some more or less aesthetic ladies and gentlemen who, deeming modern life not so cheerful as it should be, had laid their cheerless heads together and decided that they would meet every month and dance old-fashioned dances in a hall hired for the purpose.

(How similar, this, in syntax and rhythm, to the opening sentences of innumerable essays by G.K.C.) This purpose Max cannot bring himself to applaud:

> If you are depressed by modern life, you are unlikely to find an anodyne in the self-appointed task of cutting certain capers which your ancestors used to cut because they, in their day, were happy.

Just as Chesterton always rebounds after his initial skirmishes with prohibitionism, pessimism, eugenics, and other evils, so

Max rebounds into an exuberant and ample Chestertonian invention on the subject of Chesterton himself:

> If you think modern life so pleasant a thing that you involuntarily prance, rather than amble, down the street, I dare say your prancing will intensify your joy. Though I happen never to have seen him out-of-doors, I am sure my friend Mr. Gilbert Chesterton always prances thus – prances in some wild way symbolical of joy in modern life. His steps, and the movements of his arms and body, may seem to you crude, casual, and disconnected at first sight; but that is merely because they are spontaneous. If you studied them carefully, you would begin to discern a certain rhythm, a certain harmony. You would at length be able to compose from them a specific dance – a dance not quite like any other – a dance formally expressive of new English optimism. If you are not optimistic, don't hope to become so by practising the steps. But practise them assiduously if you are; and get your fellow optimists to practise them with you. You will grow all the happier through ceremonious expression of a light heart. And your children and your children's children will dance 'The Chesterton' when you are no more. Maybe a few of them will still be dancing it now and then, on this or that devious green, even when optimism shall have withered forever from the land.

The heavy-footed guzzler that Max imagined (only two years later) listening to Belloc's harangue could not possibly so dance, so prance, this new rival to the Charleston.[144]

Observe the dance steps in "Some Damnable Errors About Christmas" (for so Max renamed "Christmas Day" when in 1912 he collected and augmented the earlier set of parodies and published them as *A Christmas Garland*). It begins with the statement, pedestrian enough, "That it is human to err is admitted by even the most positive of our thinkers." It then cuts capers with that least errant of mortals, Euclid, until the geometer confesses a wild romantic devotion to the isosceles triangle. On with the dance:

> We do not say of Love that he is short-sighted. We do not say of Love that he is myopic. We do not say of Love that he is astigmatic. We say quite simply, Love is blind. We might go further and say, Love is deaf. That would be a profound and obvious truth. We might go further still and say, Love is dumb. But that would be a profound and obvious lie. For Love is always an extraordinarily fluent talker. Love is a wind-bag, filled with a gusty wind from Heaven.

All this dancing round the bush leads up to the subject of Christmas, on which mankind has been in error for two thousand years. Here the jolly girandole cuts the rug and kicks the ceiling:

> I look for the time when we shall wish one another a Merry Christmas every morning: when roast turkey and plum-pudding shall be the staple of our daily dinner, and the holly shall never be taken down from the walls, and every one will always be kissing every one else under the mistletoe.

There is certainly a lot of this sort of thing in Chesterton, who produced unnumbered Christmas pieces. The parody ends, "I shall return to the subject of Christmas next week." (The Chestertonian fecundity again.)[145]

But Max is not content simply to hit the brightly painted barn-door of Chesterton's journalistic style and ready (may I say sure-footed?) invention: he must match too his sudden modulations into gravity. The idea of Christmas as nothing but a time of jubilation "never entered the heads of saints and scholars, the poets and painters, of the Middle Ages. Looking back across the years, they saw in that dark and ungarnished manger only a shrinking woman, a brooding man, and a child born to sorrow." It is Max's greatness as a parodist that he catches the inward elusive virtues of a writer as well as his foibles and tricks and vices of style.[146]

CHAPTER SEVEN

A Last Look

Max Beerbohm and G.K. Chesterton had roughly parallel, certainly not exactly parallel, careers as essayists and stylists and what may be called public figures – Max being as vivid a personality to a small public as G.K.C. was to a large. Chesterton's life of ceaseless activity and Max's of preponderant leisure impinged on each other from time to time, quite significantly on a few occasions, as we have seen, most notably in the *Notting Hill* connexion; but we must be on guard against exaggerating either their similarities or their differences as we take a last look at the two.

The contrasts first. Max was sent away to school, and while later on he would rather think back than go back, he was happy enough there, and this Old Carthusian studs his writing with Latin and Greek tags, all learned at school, all pointed and all correct, and asserts the study of Latin to be the only avenue to an accurate and succinct English style. G.K.C. attended St. Paul's School, also a great historic foundation; it being located in Hammersmith, he was able to live at home. He read voraciously, and his friends were keen on literature and debate, but the classics never held the place in his mind that they did for Max. He did not proceed to the University but to the Slade School of Fine Art. Both of them must have set aside enormous amounts of time throughout their lives for reading; it is easy to see where Max found this time, hard in the other case. They grew up, and remained, a Thackerayan and a Dickensian, one under the spell of Rossetti, the other of Browning, one familiar with the work of Whistler, the other with that of Watts, one enjoying what may be called the ninetyishness of the Nineties and warmly disposed towards many of its figures, major and minor, the other alarmed and fearful at their aura, repute, or odour. In the Horatian spirit of *nil admirari*, Max writes in "The Fire" (1907): "There are so many queer things in the world that we have no time to go on wondering at the queerness of the things we see habitually." To this, G.K.C.'s retort must be, "haven't we just!" For him, the main problem for philosophers is this:

> How can we contrive to be at once astonished at the world and yet at home in it? How can this queer cosmic town, with its many-legged citizens, with its monstrous and ancient lamps, how can this world give us at once the fascination of a strange town and the comfort and honour of being our own town?[147]

The manifold similarities in detail of interest and expression have been occupying us for long enough. Some general observations remain to be made. Chief of these is that they are both essentially Edwardians, though both grew up (as, of course, King Edward did) in the Victorian Age, and both lived through the reign of George V, Max seeing three more reigns. They belong to that rich age (stretching the chronology a little) that gives us Bernard Shaw in his best vintages, H.G. Wells at his most inventive and most agreeable, and the crowning works of Henry James, Arnold Bennett, Joseph Conrad and Rudyard Kipling. Between the late Victorians and the High Moderns stand the two peaks in poetry, Thomas Hardy and the great unknown, Charles Doughty. No wonder that the literary alertness of two great readers who belong in their prime to this period should have dimmed after its end. As Edwardians they were untypical in resisting, G.K.C. head-on, Max with Parthian shots, its two ascendant movements; Socialism and imperialism. If G.K.C.'s doxy was orthodoxy, his ism was Distributism. Of course, neither Max in Rapallo, nor G.K.C. in Beaconsfield owned, literally, "three acres and a cow," but they both obeyed, throughout their lifetime, the right instincts about money (don't grab, hoard, speculate, or otherwise let it take over your life) and property (live on it and do the right thing by it).

Possessing thus the equivalent of their three acres and a cow, Max cultivated a contented mind – G.K.C. too, if exuberance is a variety of contentment. He was certainly over-worked in his later years, but, if driven, he was driven not by any crass cupidity but by the generous effort to complete his brother's work as well as do his own. Both were fully aware of the confusion and danger of the world in which they attempted to keep their equilibrium, whether they answered it on the flute or on the bass drum. I hasten to say again that they were unmusical, differing in this regard from Shaw and most of the writers of High Modernism: the Wagnerian revolution in the arts left them untouched, and what Baudelaire in praising Wagner called "despotic art" was not for them. This is of a piece, perhaps, with their rejection of imperialism. Finally (not as the last step in an argument; nevertheless, finally), fortunate men that they were, and children of light, neither ever had cause to doubt that he was loved, that he was loveable.

We must in the end keep them separate. They do not collaborate as a fat and a slim comedian in a comic turn: they would lead us in laughing out of court any mention of Laurel and Hardy. They do not even exit together like Auberon and Adam: they disappear into the distance, but so do all their contemporaries, and so do we all. They were not on each others' minds to anything like the degree that Bernard Shaw was for either. Shaw was the subject of one of G.K.C.'s best books, and the two men sparred with, and cared for, and advertised each other over many years. Max parodied Shaw, succeeded him as theatrical critic, and knew him well. He caricatured Shaw four or five times as often as he did G.K.C. Let us put it, and leave it, in a phrase that either Max or G.K.C. might at any time in their more than thirty years of friendship have said to the other, casually and without embarrassment, "you do me good."

Notes

In my Preface I have given reason for the rather full, though I hope unobtrusive, annotation of this study. Both writers wrote great numbers of essays and reviews, some collected promptly, some after long delay, a few not collected at all. The parenthetical dates given in my text are those of first publication, since that is usually of immediate biographical interest; the bibliographical information is in the annotation. When two dates are given for a book, they are those of first publication and of the edition cited.

To simplify the annotation as much as possible I list here the basic texts of my two authors that I have used.

First Max Beerbohm. The limited edition of Max's *Collected Works* (1924), though standard for the writings up to that date, is not complete and is not easy to find outside specialized libraries. I have therefore cited the readily accessible editions that I happen to possess. The place of publication, unless otherwise noted, is London.

And Even Now, Heinemann, 1920

Around Theatres (1924), New York: Taplinger, 1969

A Christmas Garland (1912), Heinemann, 1950

Last Theatres 1904–1910, ed. Rupert Hart-Davis, Hart-Davis, 1970

Mainly on the Air (1946), enlarged edition, New York: Knopf, 1958

More (1899), published since 1950 in *Works and More*, John Lane, 1952

More Theatres 1898–1905, ed. Rupert Hart-Davis, Hart-Davis, 1969

A Peep into the Past and other Prose Pieces, ed. Rupert Hart-Davis, Heinemann, 1972

Rossetti and his Circle (1922), ed. N. John Hall, New Haven and London: Yale University Press, 1987

Seven Men and Two Others, Heinemann, 1950. Without the two others the book appeared in 1919.

Works (1896), published since 1950 in *Works and More*, John Lane, 1952

A Variety of Things, Heinemann, 1928

Yet Again (1909), Heinemann, 1922

To these must be added:

Rupert Hart-Davis, *A Catalogue of the Caricatures of Max Beerbohm*, Macmillan, 1972, cited as *Catalogue*

Letters of Max Beerbohm 1892–1956, ed. Rupert Hart-Davis, John Murray, 1988, cited as *Letters*

J.G. Riewald, *Sir Max Beerbohm*, The Hague: Martinus Nijhoff, 1953, pp. 213–342, for bibliography of Max's writings.

Now Chesterton. The bibliography to match Riewald's for Max is that of John Sullivan, *G.K. Chesterton A Bibliography*, University of London Press, 1958, supplemented by his *Chesterton Continued*, 1968. The decision of the Ignatius Press in San Francisco to bring out the *Collected Works* of G.K. Chesterton and not simply to reprint the more popular titles was a generous one, ambitious, and I think correct, and the rapid appearance of so many important texts in both hardcover and paperback is most gratifying. The general editors deserve mention and thanks: they are George J. Marlin, Richard P. Rabatin, and John L. Swan. Editors and introducers of the nineteen volumes I have used will appear in my list.

A major editorial decision, for which I can see no justification, was to use the text of the first American edition of G.K.C.'s books and even of his *Illustrated London News* articles. How Chesterton the Little Englander would have roared at this instance of American imperial hegemonism. Sometimes the note on the text assures the reader that there are "few variations" from the English original, but what they are, or whether authorized by G.K.C., we cannot know, any more than we can know, in any specific case, whether sheets printed in England were simply bound in America or whether the type was set anew. A bibliographical shambles.

It is good to have (in progress) Chesterton's longest sustained journalism, his *I.L.N.* articles, in sequence. These, of course, must have been typeset in New York, "normally two weeks later" than the London original, in a hurry, at some risk of error. They are given their American dates, so that the Christmas pieces have January dates and the many topical references are somewhat out of date. They are indexed not by page but by date, and dated with preposterous digitality, so that 10.11.21 turns out to be 11 Oct 21. Chesterton quarried the *I.L.N.* articles for several of his collections of essays, but we are given no indication of this. If in the process he revised any of them (thereby making them the preferred text of record), again we cannot know. On the question of annotation, see my letter in the *Chesterton Review* 14 (1988), pp. 346–50.

References to the *Collected Works* will appear as *CW*, volume, page.

*CW*I, David Dooley, ed., *Heretics, Orthodoxy,* the *Blatchford Controversies*

*CW*II, *St Francis of Assisi,* G.W. Rutler, ed.; *The Everlasting Man,* Larry Azar, ed.; *St Thomas Aquinas,* Raymond Dennehy, ed.

*CW*III, James J. Thompson, ed., *Where All Roads Lead, The Catholic Church and Conversion, Why I am a Catholic, The Thing: Why I am a Catholic, The Way of the Cross*

*CW*IV, James V. Schell, S.J., ed., *What's Wrong with the World, The Superstition of Divorce, Eugenics and Other Evils, Divorce Versus Democracy, Social Reform Versus Birth Control*

*CW*V, Michael Novak and John McCarthy, ed., *Outline of Sanity, The Appetite of Tyranny, The Crimes of England, Lord Kitchener, Utopia of Usurers, How to Help Annexation, The End of the Armistice*

*CW*VI, Denis J. Conlon, ed., *The Club of Queer Trades* [with G.K.C.'s illustrations], *The Napoleon of Notting Hill* [with W. Graham Robertson's illustrations], *The Ball and the Cross, The Man Who Was Thursday*

*CW*XI, Denis J. Conlon, ed., *Collected Plays, Chesterton on Shaw*

*CW*XV, Alzina Stone Dale, ed., *Chesterton on Dickens* [includes *The Victorian Age in Literature*]

*CW*XVI, Randall Paine, ed., *The Autobiography*

*CW*XVIII, Russell Kirk, ed., *Thomas Carlyle, Leo Tolstoy, Robert Louis Stevenson, Chaucer*

CW XXI, Robert Royal, ed., *What I Saw in America, The Resurrection of Rome, Sidelights* [*on New London and Newer York*]
CW XXVII–XXXIV, Lawrence J. Clipper, ed., *The Illustrated London News*: This continuing series is complete from 1905 to 1928.

1. *Letters*, 25.

2. "Brigade" in *More*; "The Fire" in *Yet Again*; *Autobiography*, *CW*, XVI, 100–1; the verses are cited, without date, by Maisie Ward, *Gilbert Keith Chesterton* (New York: Sheed & Ward, 1943), 154. Slang changes over the years: a schoolboy rag is not a precocious publication but a romp.

3. Carlyle quoted in "Dandies and Dandies" (1893–6) *Works*, 14; Ellen Moers, *The Dandy from Brummell to Beerbohm* (London: Secker & Warburg, 1960); A.E. Carter, *The Idea of Decadence in French Literature 1830–1900* (Toronto: University of Toronto Press, 1958) for the decadent-dandy as the exact opposite of the noble savage.

4. Ezra Pound, "Brennbaum" in *Hugh Selwyn Mauberley* (1915). Will Rothenstein also uses the word *crystal* to apply to Max; *Men and Memories 1872–1900* (London: Faber, 1931), 144.

5. *Letters*, 64–5, to Arnold Bennett (9 May 1909); Max to Gosse, quoted in J.G. Riewald, *Beerbohm's Literary Caricatures* (Hamden, CT: Archon, 1977), 16: 116 for Max's notes.

6. Ward, *G.K.C.*, 61; *More Theatres*, 456; caricature listed (no. 309), dated and described in Rupert Hart-Davis, *Catalogue*.

7. *Works*, 123–4. Lane's bibliography is not included in this edition.

8. *A Social Success* is included in *A Variety of Things*.

9. Bernard Shaw, *Saturday Review* (2 May 1898); Max to Bohun Lynch, *Max Beerbohm in Perspective* (London: Heinemann, 1921), ix.

10. Max to Edmund Gosse, *Letters*, 18 (25 March 1899); epistle dedicatory to Edward Gordon Craig (1924), *Around Theatres*, vii–ix.

11. "Lytton Strachey" (1943) in *Mainly on the Air*, 194; *A Peep into the Past*, 76.

12. *Last Theatres*, 259 (11 August 1906); in an unsigned review of

Marie Corelli (26 Sept. 1896) Max refers to one Max Beer-bohm as "also intent on advertisement": *Peep*, 19; *The Man Who Was Thursday* (1908) *CW*, VI, 584.

13. Brian Reade, *Aubrey Beardsley* (New York: Bonanza, 1967) item 216, vignette (1893), and note p. 329; also his Pierrot drawings, items 397–401; Max's self-caricature (*Catalogue* 1404) appeared 1896 on the binding-case of *Twenty-five Gentlemen*.

14. *Works*, 115; *Illustrated London News* (hereafter, *I.L.N.*) Dec. 1919, in *CW*, XXXI, 579; "Milton and Merrie England" in *Fancies Versus Fads* (London: Methuen, 1923), 220–1.

15. "The Surrender of a Cockney" (1909) in *Alarms and Discursions* (New York: Dodd Mead, 1911), 16. For his place in the welter of ideas and notions and personalities centred in early twentieth-century Fleet Street, see John Coates, *Chesterton and the Edwardian Cultural Crisis* (Hull: Hull University Press, 1984).

16. His bold lines and bright colours are best seen in *The Coloured Lands*, a posthumous collection (London, Sheed & Ward 1938).

17. "The gods bestowed on Max the gift of perpetual old age," Oscar Wilde said of the young Oxonian, and kept up the joke in writing to Robert Ross (31 May 1898): "I see that Max has become Dramatic Critic, and has begun by his valedictory address. He is clearly entitled to his retiring pension by this time." Rupert Hart-Davis, ed. *The Letters of Oscar Wilde* (London: Hart-Davis, 1962), 366 n., 749. Auden's good opinion is quoted by John Sullivan in his edition of *Greybeards at Play and Other Comic Verse* (London: Paul Elek, 1974), 9–10.

18. D.J. Conlon, ed. *G.K. Chesterton. The Critical Judgments, Part I* (Antwerp Studies in English Literature, 1976), 38, for *Whitehall Review* (27 Feb. 1902); G.K.C., *The Defendant* (London: Dent, 1901, 1922), 131. For classical and Renaissance paradoxical defences, see Rosalie Colie, *Paradoxia Epidemica* (Princeton, NJ: Princeton University Press, 1966), 3–4; 25, 35, 483 and bibliography. Note however that G.K.C. in *Orthodoxy*, *CW*, I, 213, dissociates himself from "the mere ingenious defence of the indefensible."

19. "King George the Fourth" and "The Pervasion of Rouge" (both 1894) in *Works*, 50, 83.

20. *Last Theatres*, 510; centennial tribute. *Letters*, 223 n. 1; "1880" (1894) in *Works*, 46.

21. The student of Max's style should consult the studies of J.G. Riewald, *Sir Max Beerbohm. Man and Writer* (The Hague: Nijhoff, 1953) and Lawrence Danson, *Max Beerbohm and the Act of Writing* (Oxford: Clarendon, 1989).

22. *The Daily News*, 8 January 1902; he returns to the subject of Max's seriousness as a dramatic critic, *I.L.N.*, March 1908 and Sept. and Nov. 1909: *CW*, XXVIII, 67, 393, 431.

23. *Varied Types* (New York: Dodd Mead, 1903), 218; Max, "Diminuendo" (1895), *Works*, 115; *CW*, XVI, *Autobiography*, 101; *Robert Browning* (London: Macmillan, 1903, 1926), 33.

24. *G.F. Watts* (London: Duckworth, 1904, 1920), 3; Max on F.M. Brown, "Servants" (1918), *And Even Now*, 177–8; on Watts, "William Rothenstein" (1926) *A Peep*, 59; G.K.C., *Watts*, 59, 60, 69.

25. Max, with an irony that escapes me, originally called "Diminuendo" "Be It Cosiness"; see also *Works*, 70, 122. Max's *Christmas Garland* is more astringent than G.K.C.'s host of Christmas essays, but both are merry, domestic, warm. G.K.C. finds "cosiness" characteristic of the Victorian novel and the Victorian age: *The Victorian Age in Literature*, *CW*, XV, 460.

26. Max's review, "A Deplorable Affair," (5 Sept. 1908), *Around Theatres*, 516–19, ends, "Well, I suppose blasphemy pays."

27. Max's *Nineties* (Philadelphia: Lippincott, 1958) for "Mr. Gladstone Goes to Heaven," eleven drawings (1899); G.K.C, *Collected Poems* (London: Methuen, 1927), 341. It may be noted that G.K.C. defined Browning's liberalism, and his own, not in any doctrinal or partisan terms but as "a belief in growth and energy and in the ultimate utility of error": *Robert Browning*, 86.

28. This aspect of G.K.C. is well discussed by Margaret Canovan, *G.K. Chesterton Radical Populist* (New York: Harcourt Brace Jovanovich, 1977).

29. W. Graham Robertson, *Time Was* (London: Hamish Hamil-

ton, 1931), 309. In a letter to Robertson Max called it "A wholly perfect thing ... a most loving and penetrating and lovable book – bathed in fun, too": Kerrison Preston, ed., *Letters from Graham Robertson* (London: Hamish Hamilton, 1953), 269.

30. J. Lewis May, *John Lane and the Nineties* (London: John Lane, 1936); J.G. Nelson, *The Early Nineties: A View from The Bodley Head* (Cambridge, MA: Harvard University Press, 1971). Max last published with Lane in 1899 and first with Heinemann (*The Poets' Corner*) in 1904.

31. *Time Was*, 309–10; G.K.C., *George Bernard Shaw* in *CW*, XI, 404–5; *Autobiography* 100–1.

32. Reviewers cited in Conlon, *Critical Judgments*, 83–102; Ward, *G.K.C.*, 175 for Frances Chesterton's diary.

33. "A Note on Notting Hill," in *The Week-end Review* (20 Dec. 1930): 915, as cited by Ian Boyd, *The Novels of G.K. Chesterton* (London: Paul Elek, 1975), 202, n. 24.

34. "The Naming of Streets," in *Yet Again*, 193; *The Napoleon of Notting Hill With Seven Full-Page Illustrations* by W. Graham Robertson and a *Map of the Seat of War* (London: John Lane, 1904). References are to *CW*, VI (citations identified by *Napoleon* and page): this reproduces the illustrations. *Napoleon*, 274. Arteries made both men see red: Max denounces them in "Speed" (1936), a broadcast included in *Mainly on the Air*; and G.K.C. "On Mr. Thomas Gray" (1932), *All I Survey* (London: Methuen, 1933), 128: "Roads will not be roads, for there will be no places for them to go to; there will be only those ominously called arterial, and resembling, indeed, those open and spouting arteries that are an inevitable sign of death."

35. *Napoleon*, 228–9. Note that G.K.C. uses the unfriendly word "fop," not "dandy." The Max quotation, slightly altered for the fit, is from "Dandies and Dandies," *Works*, 10.

36. *Napoleon*, 231, 230. The phrase "vocalic pulchritude" is applied by the poet and artist David Jones to Fr. O'Connor, who received him into the Roman Catholic Church in 1921, the year before he received G.K.C. See *The Kensington Mass* (London: Agenda Editions, 1975), 7.

37. *Napoleon*, 256, 328.

38.   *The Defendant*, 105–110; *More*, 178–9; *Napoleon*, 262. "A Panacea" in *Around Theatres*, 334–6, imagines King Edward VII (always a *monstre gai* for Max) decreeing the closure of theatres for ten years, in similar grandiloquent style. This was 23 July 1904, a few months after the publication of *Napoleon*.

39.   *Napoleon*, 254. For Thackeray's sporting a single eye-glass as an undergraduate, see Lionel Stevenson, *The Showman of Vanity Fair* (New York: Scribners, 1947), 28; for Max, see endpapers of Lord David Cecil's biography and Robertson's illustration. The secular quality of *Napoleon* is noted by Christopher Hollis, *The Mind of Chesterton* (London: Hollis & Carter, 1970), 111. Many otherwise useful critical discussions of the novel hardly notice the Beerbohm connexion: Lawrence J. Clipper, *G.K. Chesterton* (New York: Twayne, 1974); Lynette Hunter, "A Reading of *N.N.H.*," *Chesterton Review* 3 (1976): 118–28; Joseph A. Quinn, "Eden and the New Jerusalem," *Chesterton Review* 3 (1976): 230–9; Gary Wills, *Chesterton Man and Mask* (New York: Sheed & Ward, 1961), 104–7.

40.   *Napoleon*, 276, 311, 313.

41.   *Napoleon*, 279.

42.   *Napoleon*, 284–5.

43.   *Napoleon*, 338–9. "T. Fenning Dodworth" (1922), Max's surpassingly dull pundit, appears in *A Variety of Things*, 139–59, and in *Mainly on the Air*, 176–91; Walter Pater, *Imaginary Portraits* (London: Macmillan, 1900–1), 156.

44.   Fairy tale, from "On the Innocence of Macaulay" (1929), *Come to Think of It* (London: Methuen, 1930, 1932), 170; suburbs, from *The Coloured Lands*, 107–8.

45.   *CW*, XXVII, 39; Max, *Letters to Reggie Turner*, ed. Rupert Hart-Davis (New York: Lippincott, 1965), 160.

46.   *Letters to Reggie*, 193, 194–5. The other major special collection of Max letters, *Max and Will* [Rothenstein], Mary M. Lago and Karl Beckson, ed. (London: John Murray, 1975) makes no mention of G.K.C. The letter apparently to Will is cited from David Cecil, *Max A Biography* (London: Constable, 1964), 370. *What's Wrong …*, *CW*, IV, James V. Schell S.J. ed., 35, 71. See also his preface to *Alarms and Discursions* (New

York: Dodd Mead, 1911) vi: "Some time ago I tried to write an unobtrusive sociological essay called "What is Wrong." Somehow or other it turned into a tremendous philippic called "What's Wrong with the World," with a photograph of myself outside; a photograph I swear I had never seen before and am far from anxious to see again." I include in this note, but not in my text, an instance where G.K.C. may have shot an arrow o'er the house and hurt his brother: in "The Aristocratic 'Arry" (1912), *A Miscellany of Men* (London: Methuen, 1912), 213, he writes: "If, living in Italy, you admire Italian art while distrusting Italian character, you are a tourist, or cad. If, living in Italy, you admire Italian art while despising Italian religion, you are a tourist, or cad .... Englishmen will often live a long time in Italy without discovering the nationality of the Italians. But the test is simple. If you admire what Italians did without admiring Italians – you are a cheap tripper." Max lived half his long life in Italy and never spoke the language, a fact that leaves some of his admirers, W.H. Auden among them, unamused. However, G.K.C. probably did not have Max in mind: at the time of writing. Max still had forty years not to learn Italian.

47. *Letters*, 13; *Letters to Reggie*, 275, 277. Belloc's observation of Max as among the mourners does not otherwise figure in biographies of either Max or G.K.C: Belloc, *Saturday Review of Literature* (4 July 1936): 3–4, 14.

48. *Rossetti and His Circle*, drawing no. 4; *Seven Men*, 7.

49. G.K.C.'s *Judgment of Doctor Johnson* (1927) in *CW*, XI; Max, "A Clergyman" (1918) in *And Even Now*, 231–41; on moustache, *G.K.'s Weekly* (21 March 1925): 13.

50. Quaint period, "On the King" (1929) in *Come to Think of It* (London: Methuen, 1930), 237; Max, "King George the Fourth," *Works*, 47–77; G.K.C., *Varied Types*, 91, 204; R.S.L. essay in *G.K.C. as M.C.* (London: Methuen, 1929), 214; review of Leslie, in *The Glass Walking-Stick* (London: Methuen, 1955), 74–8.

51. "On Bath" in *Generally Speaking* (London: Methuen, 1928), 118–23; "The Romance of a Rascal" (1936) in *The Common Man*

(New York: Sheed & Ward, 1950), 43, recalling Thackeray's essay "De Juventate" in *Roundabout Papers*. In *Eugenics and Other Evils*, *CW*, IV, 358, he tells a story of Beau Brummell and remarks on the nearness of vanity to humility.

52.   *Works*, 46; *Victorian Age*, *CW*, XV, 436; *Rossetti and his Circle*, 18; *Browning*, 163; E. Clerihew Bentley, *The Complete Clerihews*, ed. Gavin Ewart (Oxford: Oxford University Press, 1983), 90. In *The Victorian Age* (467) G.K.C. writes: "Mr. Max Beerbohm has remarked (in his glorious essay called *Ichabod*, I think), that Silas Marner would not have forgotten his miserliness if George Eliot had written of him in her maturity. I have a great regard for Mr. Beerbohm's literary judgments; and it may be so...." but Chesterton would rather have Silas Marner than that maturity of "analysed dust heaps," *Daniel Deronda*. The passage from "Ichabod" (1900) is in *Yet Again*, 153–4.

53.   G.K.C., *Autobiography*, *CW*, XVI, 265–6; also his essay on Swinburne (1931) in *All is Grist* (London: Methuen, 1932), 243–62, and the passage on pantheism and revolt in *Orthodoxy*, *CW*, I, 317 ff.; Max, "No. 2, 'The Pines'" (1914), *And Even Now*, 55–88. Max met Swinburne in 1899 and several times thereafter before his death ten years later, on which occasion he wrote praising Edmund Gosse for his "Personal Recollections" (*Letters*, 66–7). Gosse's request in 1914 for similar recollections prompted Max's piece. His notes are quoted from Cecil, *Max*, 208–9.

54.   *Works*, 123–4; *CW*, XI (*Shaw*) 486; *Works*, 46; *Robert Louis Stevenson*, *CW*, XVIII, 84. Early and late, G.K.C. showed acquaintanceship with Max's rather Wildean fairy tales. "Yai and the Moon" (1897) is merely mentioned in "On the Solar System" (1931), *All I Survey* (London, Methuen, 1933), 226; but in *Varied Types*, 74, he makes this interesting observation, which shows surprising finesse: "The fundamental conception in the minds of the majority of our younger writers is that comedy is, *par excellence*, a fragile thing. It is conceived to be a conventional world of the most absolutely delicate and gimcrack description. Such stories as Mr. Max Beerbohm's 'Happy Hypocrite' are conceptions which would vanish or fall

into utter nonsense if viewed by one single degree too seriously."

55. See Maisie Ward, 44, on G.K.C.'s notebook drawings. *The Flying Inn* (New York: Garden City, 1914), 123; Max's tribute on the occasion of Beardsley's death was published in 1898 and reprinted in *A Variety of Things*, 218–32. Beardsley, of course, was still alive when young Max wrote of himself as belonging to the "Beardsley period." In their caricatures of each other, Aubrey saw the foetus and the child in Max, Max the blighted child in Aubrey.

56. Pound sparred with G.K.C. from time to time but wrote a generous tribute to him in the Rapallo newspaper when he died. Eliot made the cabman quip to David Jones: see William Blissett, *The Long Conversation: A Memoir of David Jones* (Oxford: Oxford University Press, 1981), 109; William Blissett, "G.K. Chesterton and English Literary Modernism," *Chesterton Review* 34 (2008): 113–144.

57. *The Renaissance* (1893 text) will be cited from the edition of Donald L. Hall (Berkeley, CA: University of California Press, 1980); other citations from Pater's *Collected Works* (London: Macmillan, 1900–1) by title and page. For Wilde, unless otherwise noted, I have used the 14-volume *Collected Works* (Boston: Luce, 1908).

58. Daisy Ashford, *The Young Visiters* (London: Chatto & Windus, 1919, 1952), 24; *Renaissance* 106 for condition of music; 75, 93 for vagueness; Edward Thomas, *Walter Pater* (London: Seeker, 1913), 104, 219, quoting Wilde, *Intentions* 117; A.C. Benson, Walter Pater (London: Macmillan, 1906), 114.

59. Wilde, *Intentions* 103, 115; *More* 240; Chesterton's hymn, "O God of earth and altar," was included in the *English Hymnal* as early as 1906.

60. Lawrence Danson, *Max Beerbohm and the Act of Writing* (Oxford: Clarendon, 1989), 2; Pater's essay on "Raphael" is included in *Miscellaneous Studies*, 38–61.

61. Thomas Wright, *The Life of Walter Pater* (London: Everett, 1907), I, 192; R.M. Seiler, ed. *Walter Pater: A Life Remembered* (Calgary: University of Calgary Press, 1987), 2–3, 26, 62, 108

(also 66, 104, 248); Michael Levey, *The Case of Walter Pater* (London: Thames and Hudson, 1978), 171 quotes a description of his improved appearance in London, in "smart top-hat and black jacket, with stiff clipped moustache, neatly rolled umbrella, and dog-skin gloves."

62. Pater's essay on "English Literature" (1886), *Essays from "The Guardian"* 15; Stevenson's phrase first appeared in the essay, "A College Magazine" (1887).

63. *Appreciations*, 134; Symonds's letter in R.M. Seiler, ed. *Walter Pater: The Critical Heritage* (London: Routledge, 1980), 55; Michael Holroyd, *Lytton Strachey* (London: Heinemann, 1965), I, 118.

64. "The Child in the House," *Miscellaneous Studies*, 189–90; Levey 129 for morgue, 169 for Vernon Lee; *Appreciations*, 65, 199–200; *Gaston de la Tour* 67.

65. *Gaston de la Tour*, 28, 134; Edmund Gosse, *Critical Kit-Kats* (London: Heinemann. 1896), 253.

66. J.G. Riewald, *Remembering Max Beerbohm* (Assen: Van Gorcum, 1991), 102.

67. "A variegated dramatic life": Pater, *The Renaissance* in *Collected Works* (London: Macmillan, 1912), 236.

68. "Conclusion" to *The Renaissance*, 186–90.

69. *The Renaissance*, 150.

70. *Works*, 9 (compare, *The Renaissance*, xxiii, 133, 183); *Works*, 20, 47.

71. *More*, 150, 152, 192, 232–3, 247.

72. *Around Theatres*, 22 Dec 1900, 112; 24 Jan 1903, 239; *Yet Again* 104, 201–2; Lionel Johnson, *Post Liminium* (London: Elkin Matthews, 1911), 12; *Last Theatres* (15 Dec 1906): 268. Max is joking about limelight, but it has been argued, with references to contemporary science, that the source of Pater's metaphor is indeed the oxyhydrogen flame, Drummond light, limelight: see Billie Andrew Inman, "The Intellectual Content of Walter Pater's 'Conclusion'," in Philip Dodd, ed. *Walter Pater: An Imaginative Sense of Fact* (London: Frank Case, 1981), 23–4; *Around Theatres* (9 July 1904): 332.

73. *Letters to Reggie Turner*, 90; one notes the Maloryism in "how that"; one laments the absence of the exclamation point in

"Well"; Max's notes are quoted, from a manuscript in the Berg Collection, New York Public Library, by John Felstiner, *The Lies of Art* (London: Gollancz, 1973), 45; the lovely phrase "lion of milder roar" is applied to Pater by Logan Pearsail Smith, *Reperusals and Recollections* (London: Constable, 1936), 321.

74. Cecil, *Max*, 373.

75. Lawrence Danson, *Max Beerbohm and The Mirror of the Past* (Princeton, NJ: Princeton University Press, 1982); *Mainly on the Air*, 128, 129.

76. The title essay of *A Peep into the Past*, 3–8; *A Variety of Things*, 210.

77. Douglas Cleverdon, who produced *Zuleika Dobson* for the B.B.C., told me of a message he received from Max – "shrieker not hiker." On the subject of names, this may be the place to pause briefly over Ernest and earnest. Lady Bracknell opines that "German sounds a thoroughly respectable language," but Cecily knows that she looks "quite plain" after her German lesson. The first thing to say about the royal and German name Ernst, or Ernest, is that it is thorough, respectable, plain; and surely that is the first thing that Wilde and his set would laugh at. This is complicated by the appearance in 1892 of a book of poems by John Gambril Nicholson, *Love in Earnest*; the second stanza of the poem "Of Boys' Names" is this:

> One name can make my pulses bound,
>   No peer it owns, nor parallel,
> By it is Vivian's sweetness drowned,
>   And Roland, full as organ-swell;
>   Though Frank may ring like silver bell,
> And Cecil softer music claim,
>   They cannot work the miracle,
> 'Tis Earnest gets my heart a-flame.

Of the twenty names, adduced, two are those of Oscar Wilde's sons, Cyril and Vivian, but the "little Prince," Ernest, is the winner: his softness is as gigglesome as the sternness of the normal bearer of the name. Quoted from Brian Reade, *Sexual*

Heretics (London: Routledge, 1970), 301–2.

78.　J.G. Riewald, *Remembering Max Beerbohm*, 88, gives that as his stature "by his own account;" Chesterton was six-two and Wilde six-three (Richard Ellmann, *Oscar Wilde* [London: Hamish Hamilton, 1987], 26).

79.　*Dickens* in *CW*, XV, 41–2; *Heretics* in *CW*, I, 95. For Pater's crystal, see *Appreciations*, 19–20, 212, *Plato and Platonism*, 135.

80.　*Victorian Age*, *CW*, XV, 69–70; *Stevenson* in *CW*, XVIII, 80; *All I Survey* 40. Another who does not join the pack is that truculent individual Wyndham Lewis: "… 'aestheticism,' though in truth rampant and ubiquitous, is on all hands violently disowned; and although the manner of Pater is today constantly imitated, on the sly, and his teaching absorbed along with his style, he is scarcely *respectable* in the intellectual sense." *Men Without Art* (London: Cassell, 1934), 145.

81.　*Heretics* in *CW*, I, 94.

82.　E.C. Bentley, *Those Days* (London: Constable, 1940): its chapters, "At School with G.K.C." and "Oxford in the Nineties," are untroubled by the proximity of decadence; Maurice Baring, "The Nineties," *Lost Lectures* (London: Peter Davies, 1932), 91–111; Rudyard Kipling, *Stalky & Co.*, (1899) ch. 8 for the advanced and aesthetic books in the headmaster's study and the "severely Philistine study" of the headboy, "a simple, straight-minded soul," who is definitely not of Stalky's company; Julia Briggs, *A Woman of Passion* (E. Nesbit) (London: Hutchinson, 1987), 59.

83.　W.B. Yeats, "The Tragic Generation" in *The Trembling of the Veil* (1922), *Autobiographies* (London: Macmillan, 1955), 277–349. Most of what one needs to know about the literary generation is to be found in Holbrook Jackson, *The Eighteen Nineties* (London: Cape, 1913); dedicated to Max.

84.　See J. Lewis May and James G. Nelson as cited in note 30; Stanley Weintraub, ed., *The Savoy Nineties Experiment* (University Park: Pennsylvania State University Press, 1966), introduction xiii–xliv.

85.　*Letters to Reggie Turner*, 100, 102, 118; *Catalogue*, drawings no. 1779, 1783.

86. E.C. Bentley, *The First Clerihews* (Oxford: Oxford University Press, 1982), 49–50. There is also one on Pater, 32: no resemblance to Pater in G.K.C.'s drawing.

87. *Autobiography* in *CW*, XVI, 96; *The Man Who Was Thursday* in *CW*, VI, 472–4.

88. *The Defendant*, 34–5; *Heretics* in *CW*, I, 42.

89. *Shaw* in *CW*, XI, 370–1 (I have corrected the misprint of "Greek" for "Green").

90. *Victorian Age*, *CW*, XV, 516–20.

91. *Stevenson* in *CW*, XVIII, 48, 79, 80–1.

92. James Joll, *The Anarchists* (London: Eyre & Spottiswoode, 1964) gives a good account of the appeal of anarchism to writers and artists, mainly French.

93. *The Defendant*, 48.

94. *The Letters of Oscar Wilde*, ed. Rupert Hart-Davis (London: Rupert Hart-Davis, 1962). For a treatment of visual, especially colour, symbolism in G.K.C., see Max Ribstein, *G.K. Chesterton Création Romanesque et Imagination* (Paris: Klincksieck, 1981), 221–56.

95. Oliver Lodge invited G.K.C. to put himself forward as a candidate for the Chair of English Literature at Birmingham University: see Dudley Barker, *G.K. Chesterton* (London: Constable, 1973), 140; *Victorian Age*, *CW*, XV, 520.

96. The "first complete and accurate version" of *De Profundis* was edited by Wilde's son, Vyvyan Holland (London: Methuen, 1945). The "lord of language" passage is on p. 65.

97. *Lunacy and Letters*, 186–7.

98. See introduction by Denis J. Conlon, *CW*, XI.

99. Jorge Luis Borges, *Other Inquisitions 1937–1952*, Ruth L.C. Sims, tr. (Austin: University of Texas Press, 1964), 78–81 "About Oscar Wilde"; 82–85 "On Chesterton."

100. *The Thing* in *CW*, III, 171–2; *A Handful of Authors*, 145–6.

101. *The Quotable Chesterton*, ed. George J. Marlin, Richard P. Rabatin, John L. Swain (San Francisco: Ignatius, 1986); *The Fireworks of Oscar Wilde*, ed. Owen Dudley Edwards (London: Barrie & Jenkins, 1989).

102. Chaucer, *CW*, XVIII, 230; "The False Photographer," in *A*

Miscellany of Men, 235; *Uses of Diversity* (London: Methuen, 1920), 166; *The Wisdom of Father Brown* (New York: Macaulay, 1914), 92.

103. Anton C. Masin discovered and introduced this divertissement in "The Great Flute Series – Chesterton, Beerbohm and Gould," *Chesterton Review* 5 (1978): 42–7. Max refers to Gould in *More*, 226-8, and in *Letters to Reggie*, 223; Gould's caricature of G.K.C. as a Toby jug appears as a frontispiece to W.R. Titterton's *G.K. Chesterton: A Portrait* (London: Organ, 1936); Sieveking (London: Cecil Palmer & Hayward, n.d.).

104. "Express" is in *Yet Again*, 25–34; "Train" is in *Tremendous Trifles* (London: Methuen, 1909), 9–15.

105. *Browning*, 28.

106. *I.L.N.*, *CW*, XXVII, 146; XXVIII, 255, 393, 431 ("20 Nov. 1909" – that is, two weeks before that); *Max, Last Theatres*, 498 (23 Oct. 1909).

107. *Around Theatres*, 496 (18 Jan 1908); Max Ribstein, *G.K. Chesterton*, 192, on transformation scenes.

108. *Heretics* (1905), *CW*, I, 112; 172: it is this sort of observation he has in mind when he praises Max as one "whose fine and classic criticism is full of those shining depths that may be mistaken for shallowness" (*Stevenson*, *CW*, XVIII, 95); on Whistler, *I.L.N.*, *CW*, XXVII (Oct. 1907), 563; *Irish Impressions* (London: Collins, 1919, 1920), 106–7.

109. *Last Theatres*, 97–8 (19 Nov. 1904); *I.L.N.* (19 May 1906), *CW*, XXVII, 193.

110. *Heretics*, *CW*, I, 199; "The Voice of Shelley" (1905) in *The Apostle and the Wild Ducks*, ed. Dorothy. E. Collins (London: Paul Elek, 1975), 138; "An Infamous Brigade" (1896), *More*, 166.

111. "W.W. Jacobs" (1906) in *A Handful of Authors*, Dorothy Collins, ed. (London and New York: Sheed & Ward, 1953), 28.

112. Arthur Symons, it seems, began it all in a letter to the *Star* (19 Oct. 1891), which reads: "As an aficionado of the music halls, allow me to express my feelings of pleasure at 'Spectator's' second visit to the Pavilion, and his admirable eulogy of Miss Jennie Hill. But may I also be allowed to protest, in the most convinced way, against his rash assumption that "nothing is

so much like one music-hall as another music-hall...." As a "discriminating amateur" he elaborates on this. See Arthur Symons, *Selected Letters 1880–1935*, Karl Beckson and John M. Munro, ed. (London: Macmillan, 1989), 85–7. See also T.S. Eliot, "Marie Lloyd" (1923), *Selected Essays* (London: Faber, 1932); Max, "The Blight on the Music Halls" (1897), *More*, 199–204; "Music Halls of my Youth" (1942), *Mainly on the Air*, 36–46; there are many references to music-halls in the dramatic criticism.

113. "The Humour of the Public," *Yet Again*, 239–50.

114. *Napoleon*, 242–3.

115. "The Cockneys and their Jokes," *All Things Considered* (London: Methuen, 1908), 12–14: *Last Theatres* (21 March 1908): 355, (23 Oct. 1909): 496.

116. Will Rothenstein, *Men and Memories 1900–1922* (London: Faber, 1932), 31; "Laughter" (1920), *And Even Now*, 301–20, the concluding essay of the book; G.K.C. on Byron and Moore (1922), *Generally Speaking* (London: Methuen, 1928), 230–4.

117. Lynch, ix; Thackeray, "Two Papers I Intended to Write," *Roundabout Papers*, *Works*, vol. 29, ed. Walter Jerrold (London: Cape, 1904), 206; *Stevenson*, *CW*, XVIII, 88–9.

118. "Apology" in *The Well and the Shallows* (London: Sheed & Ward, 1935), 15–18; Max "touting," *Yet Again*, 257. See also G.K.C. "On Essays" (1929), *Come to Think of It*, 1–5.

119. "Lytton Strachey" in *Mainly on the Air*, 202; Cecil, 395, quoting Max: "My essays have many faults, but they have the virtue of being very closely written."

120. Quoting Bacon, *More*, 128; "Note" (on playing the sedulous ape) for the first edition of *A Christmas Garland* (included in edition of 1950).

121. Oscar Wilde spoke of Max's "silver dagger" at a party after the success of Herbert Beerbohm Tree's production of *A Woman of No Importance* (21 April 1893): see *Letters to Reggie*, 57.

122. The letter to Isaacs is cited in full in Ward, *G.K.C.*, 359–62. It appeared in *The New Witness*, 13 Dec. 1918; Max, *Fifty Caricatures*, no. 9; *I.L.N.*, *CW*, XXXII, 189.

123. *Letters*, 4; "Mr. Pinero's Literary Style" (24 Oct 1903) *Around*

Theatres, 286–90; on J.G. Huneker, "A 'Yellow' Critic" (29 July 1905) *Last Theatres*, 176–81, also 292–3 for the *coup de grace*; on Jerome, "A Deplorable Affair" (5 Sept. 1908) *Around Theatres*, 516–19. *Thursday* appeared in February 1908. G.K.C. on *Jerome*, "The Divine Detective" (1909), *A Miscellany of Men*, 279; "The Member for Literature," one of Maurice Baring's *Diminutive Dramas* (London: Constable, 1911), imagines the election of an M.P. for Literature by members of all literary clubs and societies in London: at the opening, Max, Hall Caine, Kipling, and Jerome are tied, and so each must give a speech. Max's, much the longest, is reminiscent of Auberon Quin (restore the Heptarchy, a King for Rutland); but at the end the voting goes: Jerome (elected) 333, Kipling 12, Beerbohm 3, Caine 2.

124. "Kipling's Entire" (14 Feb. 1903), *Around Theatres*, 245–9, Kipling is one of G.K.C.'s "Heretics"; in the book on Shaw, *CW*, XI, 371, he observes that "if Kipling had written his short stories in French, they would have been praised as cool, clever little works of art, rather cruel, and very nervous and feminine." "Mrs. Meynell's Cowslip Wine," (*To-Morrow* (July–Dec. 1896): 160–6; *More*, 188–9; S.N. Behrman, *Portrait of Max* (New York: Random House, 1960), 280; Evelyn Waugh, "Max Beerbohm – A lesson in Manners" (1956) in J.G. Riewald, ed., *The Surprise of Excellence* (Hamden, CN: Archon Books, 1974), 93.

125. Dwight Macdonald, ed. *Parodies: An Anthology from Chaucer to Beerbohm – And After* (New York: Random House, 1960, 1965), 324–7; also Chesterton, *Collected Poems* (London: Methuen, 1927, 1950), 46–9. A parody of an academic article, with short parodies of poets nestling in it, is "The 'TOMATO' in Prose and Prosody," in Maisie Ward, *Return to Chesterton* (New York: Sheed & Ward, 1952), 203–5.

126. E.C. Bentley, *Those Days* (London: Constable, 1940), 58–9; Ward, *G.K.C.*, 51, quoting Cecil Chesterton: "he shrank from the technical toils of the artist as he never did later from those of authorship; and none of the professors regarded him as a serious art student." Christiane D'Haussey, *La Vision du monde chez G.-K. Chesterton* (Paris: Didier, 1981), 38.

127. E. Clerihew Bentley, *The Complete Clerihews*, ed. Gavin Ewart (Oxford: Oxford University Press, 1983), 8, 9; *The Emerald of Catherine the Great* (London: Arrowsmith, 1926) facing p. 64.

128. *Greybeards at Play*, ed. John Sullivan (London: Paul Elek, 1974; *The Club of Queer Trades* is in *CW*, VI, with the author's illustrations.

129. Belloc, "Gilbert Chesterton" (an obituary notice in *The Tablet*), included in *One Thing and Another* (London: Hollis & Carter, 1955), 171. The Belloc novels illustrated by Chesterton are *Emmanuel Burden* 1904, *The Green Overcoat* 1912, *Mr. Petre* 1925, *The Emerald of Catherine the Great* 1926, *The Haunted House* 1927, *But Soft, We Are Observed* 1928, *The Missing Masterpiece* 1929, *The Man Who Made Gold* 1930, *The Postmaster General* 1932, *The Hedge and the Horse* 1936. Of the other fiction of Belloc three are political satires but are not illustrated: *Mr. Clutterbuck's Election* 1908, *A Change in the Cabinet* 1909, *Pongo and the Bull* 1910.

130. The "Jewish question" in Chesterton was most pointedly raised by George Orwell in the essay "Antisemitism in Britain," included in *The Collected Essays, Journalism and Letters*, III, 1943–45, ed. Sonia Orwell and Ian Angus (London: Secker & Warburg, 1968), 332–341, especially 338: as well as music hall skits and comic papers, "There was also literary Jew-baiting, which in the hands of Belloc, Chesterton and their followers reached an almost continental level of scurrility."

131. In *Mr. Clutterbuck's Election* Belloc jeeringly brings in changes of name half a dozen times: that is what I mean by an obsession or tic. A character in the book, William Bailey, "had gone mad upon the Hebrew race" (214–15) and in an "exaggerated and absurd" enterprise is compiling a dictionary of Jewish name-changes (224). He is a caricature, and fits what Belloc says about the anti-Semite: "Thus a caricature brings out what we unconsciously know to be present in any personality, emphasises it, and though false in its exaggeration, forbids us to forget it in the future. Thus any extreme, no matter how false its lack of proportion, is of the highest value to judgment" (*The Jews* [London: Constable, 1922, 1928], 145). Belloc seems to

condemn antisemitism, but only in order to continue in it unmolested by moral condemnation. Although Bailey is a sympathetic character with a positive role in the novel, he sends a cheque to a "Jew-baiting organization in Vienna" (301). This, in 1908, puts him in the worst of company and on the evidence of the sentence above not far from Belloc himself.

132. The Chesterbelloc's ideal of Little England as part of Great Europe left no room for Empire or Commonwealth. The reader is intended to hoot with laughter at the notion that in the remote future, that is in 1960, the World Art Conference would be held "at Toronto as the most suitable centre for the Art of the whole world to meet in." (*Postmaster General*, 86) This reader finds the joke provincial and declines to hoot.

133. Chesterton, "The Problem of Zionism," *The New Jerusalem* (London: Hodder and Stoughton, 1920), chapter 13, p 270–2; Belloc, *The Jews*, xvi. The book doggedly insists on overstating the "problem." Belloc's book on the United States has a chapter on *its* the racial problem, which turns out to be the Jewish problem, not what any sane and moral person would expect.

134. *Fifty Caricatures* (London: Heinemann, 1913), no. 9 and no. 47.

135. Rupert Hart-Davis, *A Catalogue of the Caricatures of Max Beerbohm* (London: Macmillan, 1972), gives descriptions, titles and captions, dates and exhibitions, and present location of the eight caricatures of G.K.C. alone, and cross-lists the ten others including him as part of a group or pair. Ward, 169, for comment by Frances Chesterton.

136. The "Speech" is reproduced in John Felstiner, *The Lies of Art: Max Beerbohm's Parody and Caricature* (London: Gollancz, 1972), 170; *Catalogue* no. 1423 and plate 6 for Deputation.

137. *Heretics*, in *CW*, I, 64.

138. Caption from G.K.C.'s *Shaw*, *CW*, XI, 487; after 1935 these words no longer close the book, since "Second Thoughts on Shaw" (1934) was added as "The Later Phase." See *Catalogue*, no. 1499 for "Mild Surprise"; 1492 for "Leaders of Thought"; 1491 for "Mr. Shaw's Sortie."

139. *Catalogue*, no. 314. The photograph of G.K.C. at sixteen is in Ward, 72.

140. *Catalogue*, no 121.

141. *The Illustrated Zuleika Dobson* (New Haven: Yale University Press, 1985), 40, where the sound of "two heavy boots" introduces Noaks; the Duke's feet appear to good advantage in the drawings opposite pages 200, 270, 290, Max "And only just thirteen!" in *Fifty Caricatures* (1913). Mrs. Cecil [Ada] Chesterton, *The Chestertons* (London: Chapman Hall, 1941), 1; Michael Asquith; "G.K.C. Prophet and Jester" (1932), in ed. D.J. Conlon, *G.K. Chesterton: A Half Century of Views* (Oxford: Oxford University Press, 1987), 120.

142. *Father Brown on Chesterton* (London: Frederick Muller, 1937), 45.

143. Felstiner, 141–2, for early chronology of Max on Henry James (and a good ensuing discussion); G.K.C., "The Red Angel" (1907), *Tremendous Trifles* (London: Methuen, 1909), 106; *Victorian Age*, *CW*, XV, 531. Later he found lurking in Walter de la Mare's "Seaton's Aunt" the "real literary thrill" of *The Turn of the Screw*: "On the Way of the World" (1932), in *All is Grist* (London: Methuen, 1931), 77.

144. *Yet Again*, 153–4. The Charleston can be traced to Charleston itself in 1903; it appeared in Harlem stage-shows in 1913, on Broadway in 1923 and generally thereafter. Max could not in 1907 rely on his readers knowing of it, and the resemblance of the two dances is probably accidental – or a prophetic vision.

145. *A Christmas Garland Woven by Max Beerbohm*, 48, 49, 54.

146. *A Christmas Garland*, 52.

147. *Yet Again*, 3; *Orthodoxy*, *CW*, I, 3.

William Blissett is a scholarly essayist with a wide-ranging interest in literature and the arts. His *The Long Conversation* (Oxford), an account of his friendship with the great Catholic artist-poet David Jones, established him as an authority on the personalities and communities in which literary modernism was defined.

Blissett's ability to bring literary affiliations and creative milieus to life is seen in his writings on Morris, Pater, the Wagnerian high modernists, and the mid-20th-century poets who acknowledge Edmund Spenser as a literary ancestor. Now 100 years old, he is working on two studies: *T.S. Eliot and the Vortex of Modernism* and *David Jones and the Great Misadventure:* In Parenthesis *among the War Books*.

William Blissett FRSC is emeritus professor of English Literature at the University of Toronto.

Lightning Source UK Ltd.
Milton Keynes UK
UKHW010729070223
416609UK00002B/564

9 781772 442496